THE **FORTUNES** OF **TEXAS**

FORTUNE'S JUST DESSERTS

———— ✠ ————

USA TODAY BESTSELLING AUTHOR

Marie Ferrarella

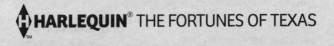

HARLEQUIN® THE FORTUNES OF TEXAS

Special thanks and acknowledgment to
Marie Ferrarella for her contribution to
Fortunes of Texas: Lost...and Found continuity.

Recycling programs
for this product may
not exist in your area.

ISBN-13: 978-1-335-68036-5

Fortune's Just Desserts

Copyright © 2011 by Harlequin Books S.A.

Printed in U.S.A.

THE **FORTUNES** OF **TEXAS**

SHIPMENT 1

Healing Dr. Fortune by Judy Duarte
Mendoza's Return by Susan Crosby
Fortune's Just Desserts by Marie Ferrarella
Fortune's Secret Baby by Christyne Butler
Fortune Found by Victoria Pade
Fortune's Cinderella by Karen Templeton

SHIPMENT 2

Fortune's Valentine Bride by Marie Ferrarella
Mendoza's Miracle by Judy Duarte
Fortune's Hero by Susan Crosby
Fortune's Unexpected Groom by Nancy Robards Thompson
Fortune's Perfect Match by Allison Leigh
Her New Year's Fortune by Allison Leigh

SHIPMENT 3

A Date with Fortune by Susan Crosby
A Small Fortune by Marie Ferrarella
Marry Me, Mendoza! by Judy Duarte
Expecting Fortune's Heir by Cindy Kirk
A Change of Fortune by Crystal Green
Happy New Year, Baby Fortune! by Leanne Banks
A Sweetheart for Jude Fortune by Cindy Kirk

SHIPMENT 4

Lassoed by Fortune by Marie Ferrarella
A House Full of Fortunes! by Judy Duarte
Falling for Fortune by Nancy Robards Thompson
Fortune's Prince by Allison Leigh
A Royal Fortune by Judy Duarte
Fortune's Little Heartbreaker by Cindy Kirk

SHIPMENT 5

Mendoza's Secret Fortune by Marie Ferrarella
The Taming of Delaney Fortune by Michelle Major
My Fair Fortune by Nancy Robards Thompson
Fortune's June Bride by Allison Leigh
Plain Jane and the Playboy by Marie Ferrarella
Valentine's Fortune by Allison Leigh

SHIPMENT 6

Triple Trouble by Lois Faye Dyer
Fortune's Woman by RaeAnne Thayne
A Fortune Wedding by Kristin Hardy
Her Good Fortune by Marie Ferrarella
A Tycoon in Texas by Crystal Green
In a Texas Minute by Stella Bagwell

SHIPMENT 7

Cowboy at Midnight by Ann Major
A Baby Changes Everything by Marie Ferrarella
In the Arms of the Law by Peggy Moreland
Lone Star Rancher by Laurie Paige
The Good Doctor by Karen Rose Smith
The Debutante by Elizabeth Bevarly

SHIPMENT 8

Keeping Her Safe by Myrna Mackenzie
The Law of Attraction by Kristi Gold
Once a Rebel by Sheri WhiteFeather
Military Man by Marie Ferrarella
Fortune's Legacy by Maureen Child
The Reckoning by Christie Ridgway

USA TODAY bestselling and RITA® Award–winning author **Marie Ferrarella** has written more than two hundred and fifty books for Harlequin, some under the name Marie Nicole. Her romances are beloved by fans worldwide. Visit her website, marieferrarella.com.

To

Kate Ellie Conrad

Welcome to the world,

little one

Chapter 1

March

Marcos Mendoza knew better than to allow his anger to show on his face. Especially in front of people who were more than family—they were his employers.

But there was no denying that he was angry. After proving over and over again to his aunt and uncle, María and José Mendoza, that he had the business savvy to run Red, their wildly successful restaurant in Red Rock, Texas, his opinion had been completely discounted. Worse, it had been ignored to the point that neither one of them had even *asked* him for it.

If they had, he would have gladly told them that hiring Wendy Fortune was as bad an idea as serving their loyal patrons five-day-old salmon.

Never mind that the twenty-one-year-old heiress was as beautiful as a Texas June sunrise, that she had long brown hair, sparkling brown eyes and a figure that could make a grown man babble like a two-year-old when it was set off to its best advantage. Marcos knew a flirt when he saw one, and this barely-out-of-her-teens woman was a flirt with a capital *F-L*. She was also trouble.

He was well acquainted with her type.

Marcos had to admit—silently—that a woman as attractive as Wendy would have definitely piqued his interest on an after-hours, social level. But as a non-productive member of his crew, well, that was an entirely different matter.

He'd been exposed to her type more than once and was well aware of the ingrained flaws that were as much a part of someone like Wendy Fortune as her high cheekbones and her expressive eyes.

The youngest sibling of the Atlanta branch of the Fortune family wasn't born with a silver spoon in her mouth—she'd had an entire place setting.

He keenly resented being saddled with this fluff of an employee just because her parents were friends with his aunt and uncle and had asked the pair to indulge them with this one favor. The productive rhythm at Red was being threatened because the senior Fortunes were desperate to teach their college-dropout daughter some kind of work ethic.

Let her be a dead weight somewhere else. Not in my restaurant, he thought grudgingly.

It wasn't as if the Fortunes didn't have a great many other businesses scattered around the state and beyond. He'd heard via the grapevine that their darling daughter had already failed miserably at the Fortune Foundation's office in Red Rock. But why didn't they send her to one of their other places of business? He'd nurtured and babied Red for the last year as if it were a beloved extension of himself. His ultimate goal was to learn all he could about the business end of running a large restaurant and then, one day, to open up a place of his own.

He'd worked hard for his opportunities, Marcos thought dourly. Someone like Wendy, a young woman born to privilege and surely demanding more of the same, couldn't possibly measure up to his standards. Every man had his breaking point—and he had this uneasy feeling that she was going to be his.

Struggling to keep his intense displeasure under wraps, Marcos faced his aunt and uncle. It wasn't often that they both came in to deliver news—they obviously knew this was not going to be received well.

And they were so right, he thought.

He leveled his question at both of them. "What am I supposed to do with her?"

Other than the obvious, he couldn't help adding silently. Wendy Fortune had "party girl" written all over her. He sincerely doubted that the woman even knew what it meant to do real work, which was probably why the foundation, created in the memory of the late Ryan Fortune, had sent her packing.

"You put her to work, of course, Marcos," María answered, employing her sharp, nononsense voice. She was apparently not happy about this arrangement, either, but indicating as much to Marcos would not help. She'd always believed in making the best of any situation. Complaining about it never helped.

This time, Marcos couldn't keep the frown from his lips. "No disrespect intended, *Tía,* but I do the paperwork on a regular basis and file it away. I have no need for a five-foot-two paperweight."

María raised a sharp eyebrow in response to the sarcastic remark. "Very funny, Marcos. If your *tío* and I decide to have a comedy night at the restaurant, I will be sure to ask you to perform." And then she softened, remembering what it was like to be young and feel that you had no say in anything that directly affected you. "I know we are asking a great deal of you. You have done a wonderful job here with the restaurant—"

Striking now was his only hope, Marcos thought. "And I'd like to keep it that way."

"I am sure you do and you will," José told his nephew, an understanding tone weaving through his words. "A man as good as you are at your job will find a way to turn a social butterfly into a hard-working ant," he said with confidence as he placed a compassionate hand on Marcos's shoulder.

Marcos knew a snow job when he encountered one. "Only saints can perform miracles, *Tío.* And I am not a saint."

María laughed. "We are well aware of that, my dear."

María looked at him knowingly. She knew

all about Marcos's reputation, both on and off the job. He had an excellent work ethic, but he was also a man who made no secret of the fact that he enjoyed the company of beautiful women. *Many* beautiful women.

"You might recall," she continued, "that your *tío* and I once took a chance on an untried, handsome young man who was more than just a little wild. We were told we should be prepared to be disappointed, but we decided to follow our instincts and not listen to the advice from well-meaning friends." She gently ran her hand along Marcos's cheek. "And, I'm happy to say, we have *not* been disappointed."

"We would like you to give Wendy the same chance," José told him.

How could he turn them down after that? They had played him.

But before he could say anything, the teeth-jarring sound of a tray meeting a tile floor on the far side of the empty dining area had all three pairs of eyes looking in that direction.

The young woman in the short black pencil skirt and four-inch heels flashed an apologetic smile in response. With the grace of a ballerina, she bent down to pick up the tray.

"Sorry," Wendy called.

"She's sorry?" Marcos said under his breath,

shaking his head. His dark eyes darted from his aunt to his uncle. "She's not even working here yet and she's already knocking things over. Think of the damage she could do if your hire her."

"We already have hired her," José corrected him. His tone, although sympathetic, left no room for argument. "She begins work this afternoon."

The tiny kernel of hope Marcos had been nurturing—that he could talk his aunt and uncle out of hiring the flighty heiress—died an ignoble death. Forcing himself to swallow the bitter pill, Marcos inclined his head, resigned.

María couldn't say that she was encouraged by the look in her nephew's eyes. "I thought Wendy could begin as a waitress."

"A waitress," Marcos echoed. *Why don't I just throw all the glasses and plates on the floor and break them now?* "Of course," he acquiesced in an amiable tone that fooled neither of the two older people. "It's your restaurant."

"It will work out, Marcos," María promised the young man she had become so fond of. "It will just take a little patience, that is all."

There was patience, and then there was patience, he thought. But he did care a great deal for his aunt and uncle and they *had* been good to him. So he did his best to keep from giving voice to his extreme displeasure. Who knew? Maybe he was wrong about this Wendy Fortune.

And, on that same note, maybe pigs would fly. By tonight.

Resigned to making the best of a bad situation, he looked across the room at his newly acquired albatross. His expression was restrained and though he tried, he couldn't keep his displeasure from reaching his dark eyes.

Wendy Fortune stood reading the current menu posted behind the hostess desk. She shifted from foot to foot, waiting for this conference that rudely—in her opinion—excluded her to finally be over.

What was taking them so long? This was already supposed to have been settled.

She wasn't accustomed to being kept out of things—at least, not deliberately and knowingly left out.

The fact that Channing Hurston had lied to her had left her incredibly shell-shocked. She was still trying, in her own way, to recover.

And to regain her ability to trust people. He'd robbed her of that, as well.

Prior to that miserable day, she had gone

about her life, blissful in her ignorance that anything was wrong. She had just assumed that Channing, the blond, handsome, Ivy League young man whom she had known forever and had been her escort since before her debutant ball, would someday be her husband and the father of her children. It was just the way things were supposed to be.

Until the day he'd told her that he was marrying Cynthia Hayes.

What a surprise that had turned out to be, she thought bitterly. Cynthia Hayes. The unimaginative dolt couldn't even pick a woman with initials that were different from his own.

She could just see it all now. Channing and Cynthia would have bland, bland children and a bland, bland existence, hobnobbing with equally bland people and calling it life.

Or some dull facsimile thereof.

It wasn't that Channing had broken her heart with his sudden, unexpected about-face. She'd never been wildly in love with him. What she had been in love with, quite honestly, was the idea of living happily ever after with a Prince Charming type. And Channing Hurston, somewhat empty-headed though he was, had filled that bill. But she wasn't devastated by this unforeseen turn of events.

What she was, she willingly admitted, if only to herself, was humiliated.

It was humiliating to be so publicly dumped. In the circles she traveled in, *nothing* was ever private, everything happened before some sort of an audience, no matter how small at the time. And word *always* spread—especially when it was embarrassing.

After suffering such a humiliation, she couldn't seem to keep her mind on her studies—so she'd quit college. There seemed to be no point in getting a degree she never intended to use. Her parents, instead of being sympathetic and understanding, announced that they intended to ship her off, sending her from one set of relatives to another because they wanted her to "apply" herself.

They wanted her to "focus."

Just what did they think she was, a digital camera?

The whole idea was absurd. She didn't need *focus*—she was a Fortune. Which meant she had one. Well, okay, not exactly her own private fortune, but the family had money, which, in turn, meant that *she* had money.

And, since she did, why did she need to *focus* herself and work?

Wendy sighed, frustrated.

Still, she supposed she was better off here, in Red Rock, Texas, than back in Atlanta, where everyone would be talking about Channing and Cynthia's upcoming wedding. And how Channing had dumped that poor little rich girl, Wendy Fortune.

There would be no escaping that kind of talk if she was back home right now.

Still, her parents could have let her go on that world cruise, or sent her off to spend a season in Europe. Paris, perhaps.

Yes, Paris, she decided, warming up to the idea. Paris, where she could buy the latest fashions and arrive back home just in time to attend the wedding. Dressed to the nines to let Channing—and the rest of their society crowd—see that he had settled for second best.

But instead of Paris, she was here, in Red Rock, for God's sake. Who names their town after a colored stone?

Wendy set her mouth hard. Her parents were decent people who meant well, she supposed, but they just didn't have a clue when it came to the needs of someone with her tastes and sensibilities.

How was she supposed to educate them when she was stuck in this town by their decree?

Wendy abruptly terminated her silent complaints when she saw the tall, dark and gorgeous man the Mendozas were talking to look in her direction and beckon for her to join them.

She wasn't exactly sure why, but for just a second, her breath caught in her throat. The next moment, she came into her own again. The little skip in her pulse was forgotten.

About time they called her over, she thought.

Wendy debated pretending that she hadn't seen the younger Mendoza's gesture in order to keep him waiting. She didn't want the man thinking he could just snap his fingers and she would come running, no matter how incredibly sexy he looked.

With an inward sigh, Wendy slowly made her way over to the three people. As she drew closer, she nodded politely at the older couple.

"You want to see me?" Wendy asked the older pair brightly.

María decided to impress Marcos's position upon Wendy's young soul. "Marcos has decided to start you out as a waitress, dear."

The idea terrified her. She hadn't a clue how to wait tables. Were they pulling her leg?

"A waitress," Wendy repeated, looking from one face to the next and then back again.

They *had* to be kidding, right? She wasn't cut out for that kind of job. And it looked like Marcos Mendoza thought the same thing.

Well, she'd be damned if she let herself prove him right.

Unable to hold it in any longer, Marcos threw up his hands in complete exasperation. He leaned in closer to his aunt, whispering into her ear, "I told you this wasn't going to work."

But rather than finally agree, as he'd fully expected, María Mendoza patted his arm reassuringly with a look brimming with complete trust.

"And I told you, you just have to give it enough time, Marcos."

Marcos frowned and shook his head. "I doubt there's that much time in the universe," he informed his aunt.

"Think of it as a challenge, then," María coaxed softly. And firmly.

The look in the older woman's eyes told him that his aunt wasn't about to change her mind. He was stuck with this. Stuck with Little Miss The-World-Owes-Me-a-Living and there was no getting out of it, short of quitting. And he wasn't about to cut off his nose to spite his face.

Marcos studied Wendy for a long moment.

The young woman probably had no idea what it was like to be hungry, or to want something so badly you put aside every penny you earned in order to save up for it. Looking at her, he figured it was safe to say that she probably hadn't known anything but instant gratification all her life.

The word *gratification* shimmered in his mind's eye, suggesting other things, things that had nothing to do with Red. Gratification of a completely different variety.

Marcos shook off the thought and silently ordered himself to get back on track.

When he was at Red, nothing existed beyond its doors. And there was nothing more important than keeping the place running well and its patrons happy.

And if he had to bend Miss Rich-and-Doesn't-Give-a-Damn into a pretzel to keep accomplishing that, then Marcos sincerely hoped for her sake that she was flexible because he intended to do just that.

"Come with me," Marcos said crisply. "I'll show you where your locker is and then we'll see about getting you a uniform."

Although, glancing at her up close and personal, he doubted whether a uniform that would fit the particular requirements of her figure was anywhere on the premises. He was going to have to put in a special order.

It was starting already.

Wendy fell into place beside him. "So I'm definitely going to be a waitress?"

"Yes," he answered tersely, "You're still going to be a waitress."

But, with any luck, you won't be one for long, he added silently, for once tapping into his rather limited supply of optimism.

Chapter 2

April

"Hell of a mess, isn't it?" Andrew Fortune commented to his older brother, Jeremy, who was throwing a travel bag with a few essentials into the back of the car they were taking on their rather abbreviated road trip. It was a trip born of necessity, not pleasure.

Drew, Jeremy knew, was referring to the situation their entire family found themselves in. He laughed shortly, getting into the passenger seat.

"Hey, just because our last name's Fortune doesn't necessarily mean that the kind of fortune we're going to run into is always going to be good."

"I'd settle for half-good," his newlywed brother said. "As a matter of fact, thinking back on things, I don't know about you, but I'd settle for just some peace and quiet for a change."

Drew was anxious to get started—and even more anxious to get back. He was also afraid that this trip might not turn out the way they hoped that it would.

"If that happened, you'd probably go stir crazy in a week," Jeremy predicted with a short laugh. And then he grew serious. Their father was seventy-five. When last seen, he'd been in great shape. Maybe he still was. In any event, it wasn't going to take two of them to bring him back. If that *was* their father the sheriff in Haggerty had found. "Listen, I can make this trip alone. You can stay behind and keep your blushing new bride company. You've only been married for a couple of months. These are the good times, or so they tell me. For all we know, this trip might just be a wild-goose chase. No need to drag you away."

Drew wasn't about to be swayed. "Deanna understands," he assured Jeremy, referring to his wife. "She wants to see the old man back where he belongs as much as I do. As much as we all do," he amended.

"You've got a good woman there," Jeremy commended, then murmured under his breath, "And with any luck, so will I. Soon."

Drew knew that Jeremy was referring to Kirsten Allen, the woman who had managed to wedge herself into his physician brother's heart. They had recently gotten engaged. "Maybe you should be the one to stay here," he suggested.

"You're not getting rid of me that easily," Jeremy told him. If this man they were going to check out turned out to be their missing father, they would most likely need a doctor, and that would be him.

"You ready?" Drew asked, his hand poised to turn the key in the ignition.

"Let's go," Jeremy gestured toward the open road.

The sheriff had responded to the missing person bulletin they had posted and said that he might have found their father in town. They'd almost given up hope when they'd found their father's sedan, abandoned and smashed, so this was definitely a turn for the better.

"Think that homeless man really is Dad?"

Jeremy did his best not to sound as nervous as he felt.

Drew hated getting his hopes up, but at the same time, he needed to be optimistic. "Sure looked like it might be from that photo the sheriff emailed. A lot less dapper and pretty disheveled, but that definitely looked like Dad's face to me. Anyway, Lily's sure it's him," he added, referring to the woman his father was supposed to have married the day he disappeared, leaving a churchful of confused and concerned people in his wake.

Formerly married to Ryan Fortune, their father's cousin, the still exceedingly attractive Lily Cassidy Fortune had turned to William in her grief when her husband died of a brain tumor six years ago. Their friendship slowly blossomed into something more. But now the wedding was on hold—indefinitely.

Drew glanced at his older brother, looking for some insight. The sheriff had said that the homeless man was distraught, saying over and over again that he needed to find his baby. "What do you think all that talk about looking for his baby might mean?"

Jeremy hadn't a clue, although, he reasoned, it might have something to do with his amnesia. Maybe the last thing William Fortune had seen before he lost his memory was the baby they had since discovered. A baby whose origins was shrouded in as much mystery as their father's sudden disappearance.

"The only baby we've seen recently is the one that was found by the groundskeeper at the church around the same time Dad disappeared," Jeremy commented. Currently, he and his fiancée, Kirsten, had temporary custody until the baby's parents could be located. There was talk that one of the Fortune men might have fathered the child, but he couldn't see how that actually connected to his father. Right now, there were far more questions floating around than answers.

Shaking his head, Jeremy laughed shortly. "Wouldn't it be something if the baby turned out to be Dad's?"

Drew frowned. "Don't be an idiot, Jer. Dad's a one-woman man and he picked Lily. There's no way he would have fathered another woman's baby."

Jeremy inclined his head, conceding the point. But there was still a glaring question left. "So why did he disappear?"

"Hell if I know." Out of town now, he stepped down on the accelerator, picking up speed. "When he gets his memory back, we'll ask him."

"*If* he gets him memory back," Jeremy cautiously qualified.

Trust Jeremy to ground him in reality. "Yeah, there's that, too," Drew conceded. "For Lily's sake, I hope this guy does turn out to be Dad and that his memory loss is just temporary."

Amnesia was a tricky condition, and if William was in fact suffering from it, there was no knowing how long it would last—or if it would ever clear up.

"Amen to that."

Drew gave him a long glance, surprised. "You turning religious on me, Jeremy?"

Jeremy's shoulders rose and fell in a dismissive shrug. "Everyone needs a little help every now and then," he allowed. "In our family's case, I think we could stand to use an extra dose of it."

This is more like it. Wendy wove her way around the tables, heading toward the ones that comprised her station. Working at Red had turned out to be a far better fit for her than she'd initially expected.

Her parents had first sent her to work at the

Fortune Foundation, located right here in Red Rock. It had taken her only a couple of weeks to discover that she was psychologically allergic to claustrophobic-size offices. She felt too confined, too hemmed in. She just didn't belong in a nine-to-five job inside a building whose windows didn't open.

Granted, out here in the spacious dining area there weren't any windows to speak of, either, but the windows in the front of the restaurant kept the space bright and airy as did the ones in Marcos's office.

That room was actually smaller than her office at the Foundation, but somehow, it still felt a lot more airy.

That probably had something to do with the man in it.

If the word *gorgeous* in the dictionary had a photo next to it, she had no doubts that it would be Marcos's.

Especially if he was smiling.

She'd seen Marcos smiling—not at her, of course. For some reason, she only seemed to elicit frowns from the man whenever he turned his attention to her. But when he was mingling with Red's patrons, he always had a wide, sexier-than-sin smile on his lips.

Despite the hectic pace during business

hours, she'd managed to observe him with the customers—in particular the female patrons—and Marcos was nothing if not charismatic. He even smiled at the kitchen help and some of the other staff.

Smiled, she thought, at everyone but her.

Boss or not, she was determined to find out what it was about her that seemed to coax those dour looks from him.

Wendy wasn't used to a man deliberately scowling at her instead of going out of his way to curry her favor and approval. All of her life she'd been the recipient of admiring looks, wide grins, broad winks and a great deal of fawning.

A lot more fawning than she actually cared for. But that was predominantly because she was her father's daughter and the fawning person usually thought that he could flatter her into getting an audience with the famous Fortune.

As if, she thought with a toss of her head that managed to loosen her bound-up hair a little.

Wendy paused and sighed. That was the part she didn't care for. She liked having her hair loose, flowing. But those were the rules. Customers, Marcos had told her when he'd handed her a barrette, didn't like finding hair in their meals.

When she'd asked, "Even if it's mine?" it had been meant as a joke, but Marcos had snapped no at her, and the look in his eyes told her that he thought she was genuinely a few cards short of an actual deck.

Obviously when God had given the man an extra dose of sexiness, He had subtracted any and all fragments of humor. From their interactions, she'd come away with the feeling that Marcos Mendoza was born without a funny bone.

Too bad, because, aside from that, the man was practically perfect in every way. But he fell short of the mark to ever have a serious chance at entering her daydreams.

A man without a sense of humor was like a day without sunshine. Not really too pleasant.

Reaching her station, Wendy smiled warmly at the people the hostess had just seated. After working here for a little more than a month, she was beginning to recognize familiar faces and learn their names.

This particular table seated six and each chair was filled by a virile, rugged-looking wrangler who appeared as if he'd ridden up to the restaurant's doors on a horse rather the extra-wide truck that was now parked in the front lot.

Her brown eyes traveled from one member of the group to another, silently greeting them even before she said, "Hi, boys, what'll it be?"

The tallest of the men held his unopened menu before him, his eyes slowly drifting over the length of her torso. "Dunno about my friends, but I'm suddenly in the mood for a little Georgia peach," he told her.

Word must have gotten around that she was from Atlanta. Either that, she thought, or her accent gave her away. In any case, this certainly wasn't the first time she'd been hit on, although it was the first time she'd been hit on at Red.

Unfazed, Wendy's eyes sparkled as she laughed. "Sorry, but that's not on the menu."

"Wasn't thinking of having it here," the wrangler answered. His grin grew wider. "What are you doing later, after you get off?"

"Not being with you," Wendy answered, her smile just as wide, her tone just as friendly as it had been before. But there was no mistaking the fact that she had no intention of getting together with the insistent patron.

"Looks like the little lady's got your number, Dave," one of his friends hooted, tickled.

"She's a feisty one, this one." There was admiration in the other man's voice.

Dave, apparently, wasn't quite ready to give up just yet.

"You sure?" he asked, catching Wendy by the wrist to draw her attention away from the others at the table and back to him. "You really don't know what you're missing out on."

"Guess that'll just have to be my loss," Wendy replied, fisting her hand as she began to yank her wrist free.

"C'mon, Dave, settle down," another one of his tablemates urged.

Before anyone else could chime in, Wendy suddenly found herself being physically moved aside and manually separated from the overzealous cowboy. To her surprise, Marcos had placed himself between them, facing the amorous customer. His rigid posture told her he was none too happy about this situation, even before she heard his voice.

"Is there some kind of problem here?" Marcos asked the man, keeping his voice even and the edge of his anger visible but under wraps.

"No, no problem," the cowboy assured him, raising his hands up in the universal symbol indicating complete surrender.

"Good," Marcos replied with a quick nod.

Turning to see who was in the immediate vicinity, he called out to the closest waitress. "Eva."

Recording an order, the woman looked up and raised a single quizzical eyebrow when she saw who had called her name.

Marcos indicated the people at the table. "When you're done over there, take this table's orders, please."

Okay, hold it, Wendy thought, growing annoyed. If he thought he could just shoo her away like an inconsequential fly just because a customer had gotten a little grabby, Mr. Marcos Mendoza was in for a big surprise. She wasn't about to be dismissed that easily—especially not since she had the impression that the restaurant manager would back her up.

"There's no need to call in anyone else," she told him cheerfully, her smile never wavering. "This is my station, I can take their order."

Marcos felt his temper flaring. He was not nearly as laid-back as he had to pretend to be when he was at Red. But exploding in front of a roomful of diners wasn't something he wanted to do. Aside from it being bad for business, it was guaranteed to get back to his aunt and uncle within five minutes. He didn't want them regretting having hired him.

The way he grossly regretted that they had hired this Fortune woman, favor or no favor.

"Then do it," he instructed tersely. Before leaving, Marcos paused for a moment to issue her a silent warning that he didn't want any more trouble from her or *because* of her.

The moment Marcos was out of earshot, the man who had started the dust-up gave her a sheepish grin. "Sorry, honey. I didn't mean to get you in trouble with your boss."

Readying the electronic board she'd been given to note down the various orders, Wendy glanced over her shoulder at Marcos's broad, disappearing back.

"You didn't." She turned back to face the men at the table. "He's had it in for me ever since I started working here."

"Anything we can do?" another one of the patrons at the table asked seriously.

"Yes," she answered cheerfully. "You can order. Now, what'll it be, gentlemen?"

This time, they gave her their orders without any further incident.

Wendy Fortune was trouble.

Marcos had known in his gut she would be. Knew it the very first time he laid eyes on her. The patrons, his uncle had pointed out after observing her on the floor the second day she was on duty, liked her.

But that, Marcos thought, was part of the problem. Some of the male patrons seemed to like her too much.

He supposed, if he were an impartial observer, he couldn't exactly blame them. She had a supple figure that caught a man's attention, even hidden beneath the wide, colorful skirt and white, off-the-shoulder peasant blouse that the female waitstaff wore. Couple that with her soft laugh and that Southern accent of hers and the men were drawn in like hapless fish in an overstocked lake.

When word of mouth about the new "knockout of a waitress" spread, business at Red started booming even more than usual.

He wouldn't have minded what was happening if—

If?

What *if*?

Was it because he was annoyed that business had picked up, not dropped off the way he'd feared when he'd predicted that the Fortune girl would be bad for Red?

Or was there something else that was annoying him about her presence in his restaurant?

Was it just that rich people in general annoyed him because he thought that they always acted as if they were better than everyone else?

In Wendy's defense—as if he *had* to defend her—he hadn't noticed her behaving that way once she'd begun working here. There was no bored-to-tears heiress drama about her. She'd listened diligently while Eva showed her the ropes, instructing her where to find the flatware and dishes, how to serve people, how to pour beer into their glasses and a whole host of things he was sure Wendy hadn't concerned herself with prior to coming here.

According to Eva, she had been a good student, absorbing everything she was told the first time around. There was no need for repetition.

Maybe it was just that he didn't like his opinion being disregarded—and then proven wrong. Because, so far, the Fortune woman was working out rather well.

After he'd allowed himself some time to calm down, he silently admitted that the incident at the table earlier hadn't been her fault. After all, he couldn't blame her for taking a man's breath away merely by standing there.

Marcos stood off to the side, watching as her table of six finally left. There were just too many maybes for him to waste his time contemplating. After all, he had a restaurant to run—all of it, not just one particular employee.

"Did he hurt you?" Marcos wanted to know when she came back to the register with the table's signed credit statement.

The question—and his supposed concern— took her by surprise. Wendy braced herself for a lecture. Whenever Marcos spoke to her, there was *always* a lecture in the offing.

"He gripped my wrist a little harder than I'm accustomed to, but no, he didn't hurt me. And I think he felt bad about it." She reached into her apron pocket and displayed a rather thick wad of bills. Unlike the payment for the meal, the men at table eight had left the tip in cash. "He got his friends to leave me a real substantial tip."

Ordinarily, she wouldn't have said anything. Money didn't matter to her. She'd always had more than enough. But tips meant that the patrons liked you and she wanted to prove to her handsome, thickheaded boss that the people who frequented Red didn't find her lacking, the way he did.

Marcos frowned as he watched her tuck the money she'd flaunted back into her pocket. It was just as he'd always heard. The rich were greedy. And the richer they were, the greedier they were.

"What do you plan to do with your 'tips'?" he asked sarcastically.

Given his frame of mind, he wasn't prepared for her answer.

"I thought I'd give them to Eva." Her words drew a scowl from him—why, she had no idea—so she added, "She's pregnant, you know." Wendy realized that she'd miscalculated when she saw the look of complete surprise that came over his face. "I guess you didn't." She pressed her lips together. Why was it she never said anything right around this man? He made her fumble around like some self-conscious schoolgirl. Wendy sighed. "Did I just get her in trouble?"

"No," he answered curtly, "you didn't."

With that, he turned on his heel and made his way straight to Eva.

Chapter 3

"Eva, can I have a word with you?" Marcos requested as he passed by the attractive, raven-haired waitress. Without breaking stride or slowing down, he added, "In my office."

The smile on the young woman's lips faded away. Her sunny face paled slightly. Taking off her apron, she hurried to follow Marcos into his office.

When she crossed the threshold, Marcos closed the door. The sounds coming from the kitchen were muted. Without saying a word, he gestured toward the chair in front of his desk.

Sitting down in the worn chair behind the scarred desk, Marcos leaned closer to the waitress before finally asking her, "Why didn't you tell me you were pregnant?"

He heard Eva catch her breath, watched as she grew even paler. Was she afraid of him? Why? If anyone had asked him, he would have said that they had a good working relationship.

Eva pressed her lips together and met his gaze nervously. "You know."

He could see that this wasn't going to be easy. She was afraid of him, or at least afraid of something. That bothered him.

"That would be obvious from my question. Why didn't you tell me?" he repeated.

Eva looked down at her hands, lacing her long, slender fingers tightly, as if that was all that was holding her together. "Because I was afraid," she finally said.

It was one thing to suspect that she was afraid of him, it was another to actually hear her say it. It stung more than he'd thought it would.

"Afraid?" he echoed incredulously.

Her head bobbed up and down. "That you'd fire me," she explained. "I mean, who wants to see a pregnant waitress waddling over with their order, right?" But even as she asked, she was watching him hopefully.

Eva had been the first person he'd hired

when a vacancy had become available, about two months after he'd started at Red. He couldn't deny that he had a soft spot for her in his heart.

Which was why her response took him by such surprise. Did he come across as some kind of ogre to her and the others?

He thought he'd done his best to be fair and even-handed with all of them—except for perhaps the Fortune girl, but that was a different matter entirely. As for his *real* staff at Red, he'd tried to make himself available to all of them so that if there was some kind of problem, they'd tell him.

Apparently he wasn't as approachable as he'd thought.

Still, in light of how things were these days, with everyone watching their back and afraid of losing their jobs—usually for reasons beyond their control—he could see where Eva might be afraid.

But if she'd just come to him with this news, he would have set her straight.

As he intended to now.

"There's only one reason to let someone go—and only one reason to fire them. The first happens when the business is losing money, which, happily, is definitely not the case here at Red. The second is if the employee is more interested in getting away with things than in getting the job done. We both know that doesn't describe you. You've always been an exceptionally hard worker, Eva."

Mentally, Marcos made a notation to look into getting her a raise. With another mouth to feed, she was going to need one.

In response to his words, Eva's breathing grew a little more even and relaxed. Calmer, she looked up at him, still a little confused. "If you don't want to fire me, then why are you angry that I didn't tell you that I was pregnant?"

"Because if I'd known, I would have seen to it that you were assigned to the smaller tables. Pregnant women shouldn't have to struggle with overloaded trays," he told her.

She'd always been proud of the fact that she pulled her own weight. Now was no exception.

"I don't want any special treatment, Mr. Mendoza," Eva protested.

"It's not special, it's just common sense. If you wind up overdoing it, carrying trays that are too heavy for you, you might wind up hurting the baby—or worse. You could wind up in the hospital—and Red would be out one damn good waitress. So it's settled," he said with finality. "You take over waiting on the smaller tables, starting now." Marcos looked at her pointedly. "Anything else I should know?"

Eva allowed a little sigh of relief to escape her lips. "No, sir."

"You need any extra time?" he asked her. "Maybe some time off to go see your doctor?" When Eva flushed and hesitated before answering him, Marcos arrived at his own conclusion: she wasn't going to a doctor. "You need to see a doctor on a regular basis, Eva. It's important for your baby—and you."

Opening the double drawer on the right side of his desk, Marcos thumbed through several folders until he found what he was looking for: insurance information. He pulled out a thick booklet and handed it to her.

"You have health coverage. Pregnancy is a covered expense. Go see your doctor. And if you don't have a doctor and find that you have trouble picking one out—"

"I have a name," Eva assured him. "My sister gave me the name of the one she uses. Dr. Sonia Ortiz."

He hoped she was a good doctor. "All right. Call Dr. Ortiz and see if she can squeeze you in this afternoon or tomorrow morning. I don't want you having any problems because you haven't been taking care of yourself, Eva."

"Thank you, Mr. Mendoza," Eva cried, tears of relief shimmering in her eyes.

Marcos flushed at her words. He didn't want her gratitude, that just embarrassed him. What he did want was for the woman to take care of herself—and the child she was carrying.

"I'm glad we talked," he told her, turning his chair so that he was facing his computer. "Why don't we both get back to work." Marcos smiled, then touched the keyboard and activated the monitor on his computer. Abandoning its sleep mode, the screen instantly grew bright.

Focused on his timesheets, Marcos barely heard Eva leave his office. There was a slight pause before he heard the door being closed again, making him think that perhaps Eva had wanted to ask him something else.

"That was very nice of you."

The soft, melodic Southern drawl made him look up sharply from his screen. There was only one way to construe the woman's words, since not enough time had passed for Eva to have filled his personal albatross in on the conversation they had just had.

"You were eavesdropping," he accused.

"Yes," Wendy said simply. "I was."

Marcos stared at her, momentarily speechless. The Fortune girl made absolutely no attempt to deny her transgression. If anything, he thought he heard a hint of pride in her voice.

She was brazen, he'd give her that. In another setting, that might have even intrigued him a little. He liked a woman who didn't act like a shrinking violet. Usually. But not in this case.

"I had to," she told him before he could demand to know what the hell she thought she was doing, listening in on his private conversation with an employee. "I was afraid you were going to rake her over the coals about being pregnant. There was fire in your eyes when you walked away and called her into your office," Wendy explained. "I figured you were either mad at her—or at me. If it was her, I wanted to be there for her when you finished reading her the riot act."

His eyes narrowed as he pinned her in place. "And if it was you?"

He expected her to cower, or at least pretend to. Instead, Wendy smiled in response. That same bright, disarming smile he'd seen her aim at the customers, both male and female, when she walked up to their tables.

The same smile that somehow seemed to brighten up a room.

It was official, he thought. He was losing his mind. Because of her.

"If it was me, I thought I'd spare you having to come and fetch me. I figured that would make you even angrier."

To his further surprise, Wendy slid into the seat that Eva had just vacated and then, without so much as blinking or building up to it, she asked, "You don't like me much, do you?"

She definitely wasn't the kind of employee he was used to. Or the kind of woman he was used to, for that matter, either.

"Whether I do or not doesn't matter—"

Again she didn't give him a chance to finish—why didn't that surprise him? "It does to me," she told him. "I'm not used to people not liking me," she said with genuine sincerity. "Now what have I done to rub you the wrong way?"

Her choice of words was unfortunate because it unexpectedly conjured up a scenario in his head that had absolutely nothing to do with their work relationship, but it did have a great deal to do with him as a man and her as a woman.

A very sensually attractive woman.

The next second Marcos upbraided himself for allowing his mind to veer off the path so drastically. It wasn't like him. Not when he was at work.

Something else to hold against the woman, he thought grudgingly.

Ordinarily, he had a great deal more control over his thoughts and his reactions, both inside Red and outside, when he socialized. He was a man who liked to party in his off hours, but not so much that he ever carelessly ignored the consequences that any of his actions might generate.

But there was just something about the Fortune girl—beyond being saddled with her— that pushed all of his buttons at the worst possible moments.

Since she'd asked a legitimate question— and he wasn't the type to shy away because he'd lost his nerve—Marcos gave her an answer.

"I don't like people who have had everything handed to them and expect that to continue for the rest of their lives." He looked her straight in the eye. And was mildly impressed when she didn't look away. She was either very gutsy, or too dumb to know what he was talking about. And he was beginning to suspect, from what he'd witnessed, that she wasn't dumb. "I also don't like people who don't know what it means to work."

Wendy nodded, waiting for him to be done. So that she could begin. "Anything else?"

"Oh, there's a lot more," he assured her, even though he hadn't phrased it properly in his mind yet. "But that'll do for now."

Wendy nodded, seeming to accept his response. But rather than get up and leave in a huff the way he'd expected, she slid forward in her chair, fixed him with an unabashed, penetrating stare and asked, "Has anyone complained about me? Has anyone told you I was doing a bad job, or not carrying my weight?"

Because he couldn't in all honesty say yes to any part of her question, he tried to approach it in a different way. "Half the kitchen staff is tripping over their feet, rushing to help you."

So now he was going to blame her for that? He had to know that was completely unfair.

"I can't help it if you hired a bunch of polite people. I never asked *one* of them to do anything for me. I don't palm off my work or expect anyone to carry my load," she told him pointedly.

But there had been more to his dissatisfaction with her, so while she was at it Wendy decided to address that, as well.

"And as for what you said about having everything handed to me, yes, I was born a Fortune and, yes, my parents are rich. And yes, I don't really know exactly what it is I want to do with my life right now," she threw in, even though he hadn't said anything about that. She assumed that one of her parents had probably complained about her lack of direction to the Mendozas, who in turn might have told Marcos.

"But I know that whatever I do decide I want out of life, I'm going to have to get it on my own, because otherwise it doesn't really count. And I also realize that the only person I *know* I can count on is me," she said with feeling.

Channing had taught her that one and she had learned her lesson the hard way. She'd put all her faith in him, expecting Channing to provide her happily-ever-after for her. When he'd pulled the rug out from under her and told her that he no longer loved her, that he was in love with someone else, she definitely hadn't been prepared to land on her butt in full view of her so-called friends. None of whom offered her any real sympathy.

While the whole humiliating experience

hadn't turned her into a bitter person, it certainly had taught her not to be so trustingly naive.

It also taught her to keep her eyes open so that she didn't run the risk of being mowed down like that ever again. One supremely humiliating experience in a lifetime was more than enough.

She straightened in the chair, giving every indication that she was ready to leave. "Now, if you don't have anything else that you feel you have to chew me out about, I'd like to make a suggestion."

Oh she did, did she? Did she think that working here for a couple of months qualified her to become his assistant? Or better yet, to take his place?

"Which is?" Marcos challenged.

"Since you're putting Eva on the smaller tables, I'd like to volunteer to take over her station."

Eva's former station contained the party-size tables. Tables that accommodated office luncheons to celebrate a promotion or someone's final day at the company. Stations like that were intended for more experienced waitresses who worked smoothly and efficiently. Waitresses who didn't drop trays.

Granted that up until now Wendy hadn't dropped a tray—if he didn't count the one she accidentally knocked over just before she'd begun working here—but as far as he was concerned that was just a freakishly fortunate streak of luck. And there was just so much luck to go around.

"We'll see," he answered.

Wendy frowned. She was still sitting in the chair, her hands on the armrests as if she had abruptly changed her mind and was ready to propel herself up to her feet. She'd thought she'd made some headway with Marcos. Apparently not.

"That means no, doesn't it?" It wasn't really a question. Marcos's tone had already given away his intention.

"No," he contradicted, his eyes narrowing slightly as he looked at her again, "that means we'll see." This just wasn't going to work out, was it? He bit his tongue to keep from saying as much. Instead, he told her, "You know, we might get along better if you didn't keep trying to get under my skin."

Wendy looked at him for a long moment, as if debating saying something. Instead, she rose to her feet. "I'm not trying."

For someone who wasn't trying, he thought, she was having remarkable success.

"Still accomplishing the same thing," he told her. The way to deal with this woman, he decided, at least for now, was to ignore her. "Now, if you don't mind, I've got some work to do."

"I don't mind at all," she told him breezily. "Maybe we can talk later to clear the air some more," Wendy said as she crossed the threshold.

Just what he needed. A threat.

"Maybe," he murmured, having no intentions of doing any such thing unless he was forced to. "Don't forget to close the—"

The door met the jamb abruptly just as he said the word *door*.

Abandoning the computer temporarily, Marcos leaned back in his chair and rocked for a moment.

Or two.

He didn't know what to make of her, he thought, annoyed.

Oh, he knew what he wanted to make of her. He wanted to continue regarding Wendy Fortune as a spoiled, self-centered little brat because the negative view helped him block out an utterly annoying growing attraction he was becoming increasingly aware of. An attraction to the woman that was completely undesired on his part. But he had to admit, however grudgingly, that spoiled, self-centered, selfish little brats didn't give away their tips to their less fortunate coworkers without asking for something in return.

They also didn't eavesdrop because they wanted to make sure a coworker wasn't "raked over the coals" because they'd had a slip of the tongue. Moreover, they didn't wait around to offer comfort to said coworker.

Wendy Fortune was a damn enigma, a confounding puzzle. Ordinarily, he'd just put her out of his mind, dismiss her as not worth the time nor the effort to try to solve that puzzle.

But the fact was that she was *his* puzzle, assigned to him by an uncle and aunt who were much too softhearted for their own good—and his. And he wanted to tell them so, but it wasn't his place.

Putting up with the heiress was apparently part of his new job description.

Marcos frowned to himself.

He was spending way too much time and energy thinking about this woman and trying to figure her out. There was *nothing* to figure out. She was the devil, plain and simple, sent to torment him. She was here just to throw him off, lull him into complacency.

Even the devil was capable of a good deed every century or so, Marcos reasoned. That didn't mean he wasn't the devil. And just because Wendy Fortune gave away her tips, something she undoubtedly viewed as small change, to someone who needed every penny didn't change the fact that she still had enough faults to fill up the Grand Canyon. The sooner he was rid of her, the better.

Chapter 4

The black leather sofa creaked and sighed as Flint Fortune shifted his long frame.

So here he was, back in Red Rock again. That made twice in the space of less than four months, Flint thought. Back in January he'd come to attend his uncle William's wedding—otherwise known as the wedding that wasn't, he thought wryly. Just before the ceremony, his uncle vanished. A search of the premises turned up nothing—except his car was gone.

At first, everyone thought that the man had just gotten cold feet—everyone, that is, except for his intended bride. Lily Cassidy Fortune, his uncle Ryan's widow, never once wavered or gave in to the rumors that the widower who was supposed to pledge his heart and his honor to her that morning had surrendered to last-minute jitters and left her at the altar.

When Uncle William's smashed up vehicle was discovered, she held on just as fast to the belief that he was out there somewhere, alive and in need of help. Eventually, she got everyone else to see her way, too.

Flint felt a touch of envy. Women like that were rare. He ought to know. The woman he'd briefly married belonged to the majority of the female population. Once the I dos were over, it had become clear to him that Myra had married him to change him and make him over into the man she'd thought he should be, rather than loving the man he was.

Now, thankfully, she was in his past, as was the notion that marriage was something he aspired to. He was perfectly happy just the way he was. Single and determined to remain that way.

Which made his return to Red Rock kind of ironic. He'd come back to take a paternity test. The little guy who was currently in Jeremy and Kirsten's care was said to possibly be a Fortune. Which meant that one of them could be the baby's father. Right now, nobody knew who that was and they were involved in a process of elimination.

Although he had no desire for ties, it wasn't right just to let that baby be sent off to an orphanage. If the little guy was a result of one of his own amorous encounters, then he was prepared to step up.

Prepared—but not happy about it.

Frustrated, Flint tossed aside the magazine he'd been thumbing through since he'd signed in at the lab's front desk. He hadn't seen a single word on any of the magazine's pages.

The door on the far end of the lab's outer office opened and out came a young woman wearing a white lab coat over her dark skirt and white button-down blouse. Glancing around the room, she spotted him.

"We're ready for you now, Mr. Fortune," the technician announced.

Flint unfolded his five-foot-eleven frame from the sofa and stood up.

He silently followed the young woman into one of the smaller rooms that lined the back wall, fervently hoping to be vindicated.

"You *what?*"

Marcos stared incredulously at his brother, Rafe Mendoza, who had just popped into his office unannounced.

Older by two years, Rafe, a dynamic corporate lawyer, already had a successful law practice in Ann Arbor and was now working in San Antonio. His new practice was so successful that earlier this year he'd decided to open a second office right here in Red Rock. He'd only been back in his hometown a couple of months, but had just purchased the old Crockett building downtown, putting the wheels in motion for a new branch.

"I said that I'd like to hold the wedding reception here at Red. Is that possible?"

"A wedding reception," Marcos echoed. "*Your* wedding reception."

Marcos found that his brain was stuck in first gear, not letting any of his thoughts move forward. In the last ten years, ever since his brother had broken up with his high-school sweetheart, he'd lived a life that every bachelor—and a lot of married men as well, probably—viewed with unabashed envy.

"You're getting married."

Rafe slid forward in his chair, peering more closely at Marcos. "You been dipping into the cooking sherry a little too much, little brother?" he wanted to know, amused. "Catch up, Marcos," he urged. "Yes, in order to have a wedding reception, you have to get married first. And I'm getting married."

Marcos was having a great deal of trouble wrapping his head around the concept. "To Melina Lawrence?"

Rafe and Melina had been the ideal couple in high school, the couple everyone else aspired to be: the jock and the cheerleader, the king and queen of the homecoming dance. There wasn't a single person who hadn't expected them to get married once they graduated college.

But life had a way of intervening, of creating circumstances that divided Melina's loyalties between pursuing her own dreams, which were tied to Rafe's, and being there for the family that, as it turned out, desperately needed her.

Melina chose the latter, which in turn led to some hard feelings between them. She and Rafe broke up. That was all that Rafe ever said on the subject, and his brothers knew better than to ask for any more details than Rafe was willing to volunteer.

"So." Rafe grew more serious. "Can you accommodate me?"

Was he kidding? Marcos would move heaven and earth if he had to. "Hey, you're my big brother, leave it to me."

"I haven't told you the date yet," Rafe pointed out.

Marcos shook his head. "Doesn't matter. You'll have your reception. I know Aunt María and Uncle José would have my head if I didn't close Red down for this private party. You know how Aunt María is about seeing us all married off."

Yes, he knew. It was his aunt's life goal. Rafe laughed. "Now that I'm officially out of the picture, that'll give her more time to work on you."

So far, Marcos had managed to escape his aunt's attention. The woman probably knew a hopeless case when she saw one, he speculated. Besides, work was his primary focus. He didn't have time to wine and dine a woman on an ongoing basis to win her heart. When he came right down to it, no woman's heart was as important to him as his career.

"She can work all she wants," Marcos told his brother, then fell back on the standard excuse rather than talk about his dedication to forging a career, even though the old Rafe would have understood. But the old Rafe didn't have stars in his eyes the way this one did. "I'm having too good a time being free."

"I used to say the same thing," Rafe acknowledged. He looked more closely at his younger brother. "I didn't mean it, either."

Rafe's so-called confession made Marcos feel uneasy. "That's what makes us different, brother. I do." Marcos pulled over the old-fashioned desk calendar he kept, a gift from his aunt. "Okay, so do you have a date yet?"

"I'll have to get back to you about that."

"Fine." He pushed the calendar back again. "You know where to find me."

About to leave, Rafe opened the office door and then paused in the doorway. "I thought I saw Wendy Fortune outside in the courtyard, waiting on tables," he said, mentioning the more exclusive part of the restaurant. He'd heard around town that her parents were trying to instill a work ethic in her. He also knew that Marcos didn't like playing babysitter. "How's that working out for you?"

Marcos's expression instantly soured. "It's not. Damn woman is like a burr under my saddle."

Rafe's grin all but split his face. "Uh-oh."

Marcos looked at his brother sharply. Filial camaraderie was temporarily placed on hold. "What 'uh-oh'?" he asked sharply.

"Nothing," Rafe answered innocently, a ruse that Marcos wasn't buying. "Just, that's the way it usually starts." And then he stated the obvious. "She's a really beautiful girl."

Marcos narrowed his gaze. "You're getting married. You're not supposed to notice things like that."

"I'm getting married, not blindfolded," Rafe said with a laugh. He grinned as he walked out. "Keep me posted."

"Nothing to post you about," Marcos called after his brother.

"Congratulations. I hear you're getting married. I hope you two are very happy." The unmistakable Southern drawl coming from just outside his office had Marcos on his feet and making for the doorway in less than a heartbeat.

He was in time to see his brother exchanging a few words with the woman they had just been talking about. He was also in time to catch Rafe's knowing look as his brother glanced in his direction just before he finally made his way out of the restaurant.

"Your brother is really nice," Wendy commented, then turned around to face Marcos.

"How is it you seem to have your ear pressed against my door every time it's closed?" he wanted to know.

"At no time was my ear pressed, and it's not every time," she corrected him cheerfully.

"Then what were you doing, lurking outside my office?" he challenged.

"I wasn't lurking," she protested, resenting his choice of words. She'd come to volunteer to do a good deed. "I came to tell you something."

He felt his stomach suddenly tighten. Now what? "And that is?"

"Eva's feeling really, really queasy this morning," she said. "I told her to go home." She saw the flash of surprise in his eyes, instantly followed by more than a little annoyance. "I just figured you wouldn't want her getting sick in front of our customers. Was I wrong?"

How could he argue with that? She was right, damn it. "No, I wouldn't, but that decision is mine to make," he told her tersely. "Not yours."

She dug in stubbornly. "But if Eva came to you and said she wasn't feeling well, you'd make the decision to send her home, right?"

The answer to that was yes, but he didn't want to admit that to her. He just *knew* it would encourage Wendy to be even more impetuous than she already was.

Yes, they had more patrons because of her.

Men poured in every day until it was practically standing room only in the dining room. But that still didn't give her the right to usurp his authority or take it upon herself to try to run things.

"Do you lie awake at nights thinking up ways to annoy me, or does it just come naturally to you?" he asked.

Rather than becoming contrite—or combative, which was more her speed—Wendy smiled. That sunny, radiant smile that cleared out all the clouds in the sky and made a man glad just to be alive.

At this point, he had to admit to himself that, as annoying as it was, he was attracted to her.

How the hell could he be attracted to someone who drove him crazy like this? Someone who inherently he didn't even like?

It just made no sense to him.

But he was beginning to learn that things didn't have to make sense, especially when they concerned Wendy.

"I don't know," Wendy answered, then, in her impossibly lyrical voice, added, "I'm not *trying* to annoy you."

"Well, for someone who's not trying, you're doing a damn good job."

This wasn't getting him anywhere. Struggling, he managed to get himself under control and focus on the bottom line in this case—what Eva's absence meant to the restaurant today.

"I'm going to have to get someone to cover for Eva this afternoon."

Marcos was only thinking out loud. He hadn't meant to share the thought with Wendy. He especially hadn't meant for her to think he was asking for her help.

But in the next moment, she was volunteering. So much for being able to hold being lazy against her.

"I can do it," she told him. It was, actually, the second part of what she'd come to tell him, that she was going to be taking Eva's tables for her, as well as waiting on her own.

Marcos looked at her for a long moment. Had she forgotten about her own tables? In an effort to get her to throw in the towel and quit, he'd given her more than the usual number of tables to wait on.

"You're already on duty," he pointed out.

"I know. I can just add her tables to mine," she told him.

"Twice the work," he repeated. Was she comprehending this? "You're telling me that you're willing to double your load?"

Her slim shoulders rose and fell in a careless gesture. Her blouse slipped off her left shoulder, exposing a creamy expanse of flesh. She appeared to be completely unself-conscious about it.

He wasn't. Which was why he forced himself to focus on her face. Not that he didn't find her face compelling as well, but at least it didn't fire up his imagination the way her exposed expanse of shoulder seemed to.

"You're not that good a waitress," he pointed out flatly.

If his goal was to hurt her feelings, he'd succeeded, but she refused to let on. Never let them know you're vulnerable—a lesson her father had instilled in her over and over again from a young age.

She was beginning to realize that the man had had some wise insights.

"Maybe this'll make me a better one," she answered with cheerful determination. Her wide, bright smile never dimmed. "You never know."

There was that grin again, he thought, annoyed. Intrigued despite himself. It was wider this time. When she continued looking at him like that, he felt compelled to find out more about her, to lose himself in her alluring gaze....

But he refused to get sucked into another discussion with this woman. He knew when he was outmatched, and Wendy Fortune had a way of weaving her words around a man until he couldn't tell his left hand from his right or up from down.

And he had no desire to be disoriented.

Marcos retreated to his office while he was still ahead. Or at least breaking even.

"By the way," she called after him. His shoulders stiffened as he paused without turning around, waiting. "Congratulations on your brother's engagement."

"Yeah. Thanks," was all he said before he closed the door behind him.

Better him than me, he added silently as he went to his desk.

Wendy walked back to the dining area, smiling to herself.

She was wearing down Marcos, she could feel it. He wasn't nearly as terse as he had been when she'd first come to work here.

Moreover, working at the restaurant had turned out to be more fun than she'd expected it to be. She liked the people, liked the energy she felt when they were busy.

And when the doors were closed and the kitchen staff was getting ready for the evening shift, it was even better. She'd made a discovery the second week she was here that she'd been heretofore unaware of. She discovered that she liked to cook, something she'd never had a need to do before. Growing up, there'd been a cook, Elise, who'd made all their meals. Wendy hadn't even been allowed to stay in the kitchen when the woman was working. Elise had claimed it threw her off.

Enrique, the main chef at Red, had allowed her to dabble a little and had given her a few basic pointers, encouraging her to experiment and to trust her instincts.

Trust her instincts.

Now, there was something no one had ever said to her before. Probably because no one thought she had any instincts to speak of.

That was part of the reason she liked being here. The people who worked at Red treated her like a regular person. They saw her as Wendy the waitress, not as Wendy the heiress, and they treated her accordingly.

Except for Marcos Mendoza. Despite her

enthusiasm on the job, he clearly thought she was spoiled and incapable of doing an honest day's work.

It would be her pleasure to prove him wrong.

Chapter 5

Every day Red closed its doors at two and opened them again at five. The hours between lunch and dinner afforded the staff time to clean up from the first service and prepare for the second. While it was not a time to kick back, the stress level was notably reduced and conversations of no particular consequence drifted through the air.

Three-thirty would usually find Marcos making his way into the kitchen to check on the progress of the dinner preparations. As with any good restaurant, Red had several items on the menu that never changed, long-standing customers favorites. There were people who frequented Red specifically to order these items. Changing them would upset the clientele.

But it was also a given that if Red was to continue to thrive and grow, the menu had to keep evolving. And that meant trying out different dishes, all in keeping with the Tex-Mex flavor that Red was known for.

So, new dishes were periodically given a trial run to see how the patrons responded to them. Things that worked or secured a devoted following remained on the menu. Things that didn't were removed.

Marcos supervised the menu, but its creation and content were all up to Enrique Montoya, a somewhat temperamental but highly regarded chef who Marcos had managed to lure away from Etienne's, a pricey and popular restaurant in San Antonio.

From the very beginning, the staff, Marcos had noted, would tiptoe around the chef each morning until they could ascertain what kind of a mood Enrique was in. If he was in a genial, friendly mood, the staff relaxed and work flowed. But if the chef was quiet, speaking only in clipped, two-to three-word sentences, everyone was subdued, doing their best to be silent and not set off the somewhat volatile man.

Sometime within the first couple of weeks that he had become saddled with Wendy, it had occurred to Marcos that the chef, whom both his aunt and uncle regarded as a wonderful addition to their restaurant, would ultimately be the perfect solution to his Wendy Fortune problem.

It was only a matter of time before she would subject the renowned chef to her endless chatter and drive him crazy, Marcos thought. When that happened, he was fairly certain that Enrique would demand that a choice be made—either Wendy would have to go or he would.

And that, Marcos thought cheerfully, would be no contest.

So he waited.

And hoped.

And, one fateful April afternoon when he walked into the kitchen to check on the menu, for a brief shining moment Marcos thought that he was finally going to get his wish.

The kitchen was partially empty. A couple of the assistant cooks as well as the dishwasher—a man, not a machine, because his aunt and uncle believed in hiring as many people as they could while still making a reasonable profit—were in the immediate vicinity.

As was Wendy.

Rather than working in the dining room or on the patio doing some last-minute set up for dinner, Wendy was standing in front of one of the industrial gas stoves. Her back was to him and at first Marcos couldn't make out what had caught her attention.

Crossing over to the massive stove, he circumvented it partway until he could see exactly what the woman was up to.

The burner's blue flame was licking the bottom of the three-quart cast iron pot that she was working with. Plumes of steam were rising up from the pot and she was vigorously stirring its contents.

She seemed oblivious to his presence, although he did see the corners of her mouth curve ever so slightly. For a moment, he just stared at her, at her mouth. And then he roused himself, refocusing his mind.

"What are you doing?" he asked her evenly.

Wendy slanted an amused glance in his direction. "I guess I'm not doing it right if you have to ask." She flashed a completely unselfconscious smile at him and announced, "I'm cooking."

He frowned. Since she'd come to work at

Red, he'd been frowning more than he ever had before in his life. "I can see that."

Her expression was nothing if not total innocence. It almost drew him in. "Then why did you ask?"

Mentally, he counted to ten, found it wasn't high enough to calm him down, so he counted another ten before speaking.

"There seems to be some confusion here. You were hired to wait on tables. Waitresses do not take it upon themselves to mess around in the kitchen. It's not part of their job description," he ended sharply.

Wendy listened to him patiently, waiting for him to finally stop. When he did, she told him, "I'm on my break."

How the hell was that an excuse? "That still doesn't give you the right to run amok in Enrique's kitchen. If he saw you—" Marcos did his best to make it sound like a warning and not reveal that he was hoping for a confrontation.

"But I do see her," Enrique said, coming out of the huge freezer carrying a vat of cream ready to be whipped. Surprised, Marcos whirled around to look at the man just in time to see him set the vat down on the counter. "I am the one who told her she could experiment." Coming around to Wendy's side, Enrique paused to taste a sample of the chicken dish she was working on. Looking pleased, he took another taste, and then a third. Retiring the spoon to the side, the chef nodded his head in approval. "It is good." He eyed her for a moment. "Are you sure you never cooked before?"

"Perfectly sure," Wendy answered, pride shining in her eyes. She wasn't accustomed to *real* compliments. "Elise, our cook, wouldn't let me anywhere *near* the kitchen."

The hard-boiled, temperamental chef looked at the man who had hired him away from what Enrique considered to be the finest restaurant in San Antonio. "I congratulate you, Marcos. She is a natural."

Yeah, a natural at being a pain in the butt.

There was absolutely no reason to congratulate him, Marcos thought. To offer condolences, maybe, but not to congratulate him.

He needed to set the chef straight.

"Can I have a word, Enrique?" Marcos requested, motioning the shorter man to the side, away from the others. Away from Wendy.

"Of course." Enrique paused long enough to place his hands on Wendy's shoulders, giving them what amounted to a little bonding squeeze. "Keep up the good work, Wendy.

Next I want you to try your hand at desserts. Something special," he emphasized.

Turning around, the chef focused his attention on Marcos. Enrique joined the manager in an alcove created by a wall and the side of one of the stoves.

"What seems to be the problem?" Enrique wanted to know. The tone of his voice said that he didn't appreciate having his routine interrupted.

Knowing that, Marcos wasted no time and got right to the point. "Since when do you take one of the staff under your wing?" he asked.

It went against everything he had ever heard and observed about the chef. The man was not known for being charitable or warm and toasty.

Until now.

"I've told everyone that you're not to be disturbed," Marcos told the chef. "And that they should respect your wishes to keep a quiet kitchen if that was the way you wanted it."

Enrique inclined his head. He wasn't oblivious to the conditions at work. "And I appreciate that," he told Marcos.

Marcos noticed that, even as he spoke, the chef was looking across the room, watching what Wendy was doing. Watching perhaps a little *too* closely.

Which made him think of something else.

"Enrique, is there something going on that I should know about?" Marcos asked.

"Only that you are wasting a gifted person, making her carry heavy trays around. For all her inexperience, the young lady has taken to cooking faster than anyone I have ever known, with the exception of myself, of course," Enrique qualified.

"Now, she is not going to be as good as I am—there is room for only one Enrique." If it was possible to say something so self-promoting without sounding pompous, the man had somehow managed to carry it off. "But she is still going to be very, very good. I would pay closer attention to her gifts if I were you." And then the older man paused. "But I think you may already be doing that, yes?"

Marcos squared his shoulders, his posture growing more rigid. "I'm not sure I know what you're talking about."

"Oh, I think you do," Enrique contradicted with a knowing smile. "Which is why this whole thing confuses me. You are being very hard on her. Why is that, Marcos?"

He would think that would be self-evident. "I'm just trying to get a full day's work out of her."

"In half the time?" Enrique challenged, then held up his hands as if he was pushing away an invisible wall. "You do not owe me an explanation," he assured the restaurant manager. "But I think that you might owe one to yourself." When Marcos looked at him quizzically, he clarified. "Examine *why* you are being so hard on her, Marcos. This is not like you."

There was no need for self-examination, Marcos thought. "I'll tell you why I'm leaning on her." He deliberately avoided saying that he was being hard on her. He wasn't chaining the woman to the wall. She was free to leave anytime she wanted. And personally, he was rooting for that. "I don't like people who think they deserve a free ride just because they happen to be rich, or related to someone who's rich."

Enrique looked unconvinced, as if he knew there was more to it than just that. "I think you are being unfair. But that is between you and your conscience." The chef drew in a breath, as if preparing to terminate this little sidebar of a meeting. "Now, if you have nothing else to share with me, I have a student waiting," he said glibly, gesturing toward Wendy.

He turned his back on Marcos and crossed back to the stove and Wendy. "All right," Enrique said in a cheerful voice, a tone that no one in the kitchen could recall ever having heard from him before, "let me see what you have managed to come up with."

Marcos turned on his heel and left the kitchen.

Needing to clear his head, he kept on going until he reached the front doors. He pushed them open and went outside. Maybe some fresh air would help.

It didn't.

The thoughts that were ambushing him inside the kitchen did the same when he was outside. He couldn't seem to shake them or leave them behind.

Terrific, he thought darkly.

Frustrated, Marcos dragged his hand through his hair. Just what kind of power did this flighty girl have over people? He'd never seen Enrique so docile, so friendly before.

The thing about the chef was that he was equally surly to everyone, making no distinction between people who struggled to hold body and soul together and those who were comfortable or even wealthy. Just what was there about Wendy Fortune that made everyone else respond to her positively?

Everyone but him, anyway.

And why, he wondered, reflecting on what

Enrique had said to him, did she keep getting under his skin? It went beyond what he'd referred to as her air of entitlement.

Marcos found himself growing unduly agitated every time he heard the first strains of that smoother-than-molasses Southern drawl.

Marcos frowned.

He didn't like what Enrique had implied. He'd always thought of himself as being hardworking and, above all, fair. Maybe he was too much of the former and not enough of the latter with Wendy.

That was another thing to hold against her, he suddenly realized. Ever since she'd shown up, he found himself second-guessing himself and overanalyzing his every move. Wendy Fortune had definitely shaken up his world—and he didn't like it.

The wind picked up, making the newly sprouted leaves on the trees rustle madly.

One thing was for damn sure, he wasn't going to solve anything out here, engaged in a mental Ping-Pong game with himself.

Blowing out a frustrated breath, he pulled open the massive front door. Avoiding the kitchen—and the sight of Wendy—Marcos went straight to his office and closed the door.

It was only when he started crossing to his desk that he noticed it.

A tall, slender crystal parfait glass delicately set on a dessert plate, an extra-long spoon placed invitingly beside it. Some sort of light, creamy white confection was inside the glass, topped off with a fluffy cloud of whipped cream.

A peace offering of some sort from Enrique?

He didn't think that an apology was part of the man's makeup—he doubted that the man had ever so much as once entertained the idea that he might be even marginally wrong about *anything*—but maybe this was the chef's way of doing it.

Pulling out his chair, Marcos sat down and then looked at the parfait glass. More specifically, the dessert within the parfait glass. Cool and tall, it was a thing of beauty, a feast for the eye.

Now, he thought, let's see if it's a feast for the mouth, as well.

He drew the parfait glass close to him, sank the spoon in through the whipped cream and scooped up a taste of the concoction beneath it.

Marcos's eyes fluttered shut, an automatic response to the pleasure that permeated through his entire mouth as the flavors registered with his taste buds.

It was light, tantalizing and possibly one of the best things he'd sampled in a long time.

Intrigued, Marcos attempted to identify the different components that stirred his palate.

Was that a hint of rum accenting the vanilla, or the other way around? He was pretty certain that there was rice involved, somehow mimicking the texture of ice cream.

All in all, he found the experience incredibly enjoyable. So enjoyable that he took another taste, and then another.

Before he realized it, the parfait glass was empty and he was craving more.

This definitely belonged on the menu, he thought. Tonight, if they had enough of the ingredients to produce this on a large scale. If not, then tomorrow night for sure.

It needed a name, he thought, wondering if Enrique had come up with one. Most likely, knowing the man, he had. Marcos had never known the chef to be unprepared in any department.

On the small, outside chance that the exceedingly creative chef had neglected to christen his new creation, Marcos thought a moment. As if inspired, a name popped up in his mind.

Heavenly Sin.

It seemed appropriate because, while he didn't doubt that the dessert was sinfully caloric, tasting it was pure heaven.

Abandoning the parfait glass on his desk, Marcos left the office and went into the kitchen.

Enrique was there, frying something in one of the larger pans. The high flame beneath it was hissing and sizzling as pats of butter swiftly dissolved, ready to enhance whatever he dropped into the pan next.

"That was fantastic," Marcos cried, striding toward the chef.

Enrique looked over toward him, a quizzical look on his face.

"That dessert you left in my office—sheer genius," Marcos enthused. "Do you have a name for it yet? Most likely you do," he said, answering his own question. "What do you call it?"

"Wendy's," the chef said simply, a very amused smile on his thin lips.

Marcos stared at the man, a little dumbfounded, as well as confused.

Was Enrique saying that he'd named that wondrous dessert after the Fortune girl?

"I don't understand. Why would you call it Wendy's?" Marcos wanted to know.

"Because I'm the one who made it," said the soft Southern drawl coming from behind him.

Chapter 6

Wendy.

The slight whiff of the perfume she always seemed to wear announced her presence in the vicinity even before he heard that annoyingly lyrical Southern drawl of hers.

Marcos turned to face her. "You made the dessert." It was not a question so much as a statement of disbelief.

"Yes."

Separated by a couple of feet, Marcos studied her for a long moment. Her gaze met his, blatantly returning his stare. Marcos frowned, doing his best to look distant and unapproachable, mainly because he would have preferred being neither. And *that,* as far as he was concerned, was totally unacceptable. After all, he was her boss, not to mention that he was older than she was and that they came from two totally different worlds. His people had to work for everything they had, hers had been born with silver spoons in their mouths. Anything he might have even vaguely entertained was doomed before it ever unfolded—he just had to make certain that it didn't even try. The best way he knew how to do that was to make her want to quit.

"All right," Marcos allowed gamely, "you made this." If it was to appear as an insert on the menu tonight, he needed to give credit where it was due. "So what cookbook did you get it from?"

Her shoulders seemed to square themselves and he had the distinct impression that he was in the presence of a soldier prepared to go off into battle.

An unbidden shiver of anticipation went through him. He didn't bother exploring why.

"I didn't," Wendy informed him with just a touch of pride in her voice.

Frustrated, Marcos dropped his kid-gloved treatment. "You're actually standing there, telling me that you just came up with this dessert today."

"If that's what you're asking me," Wendy replied, "then yes, that's what I'm telling you. I just came up with this dessert."

"I told you she was good," Enrique chimed in. The pride in his voice was unmistakable, as if he'd been mentoring her these last few weeks. Which, it now seemed, he had.

"Yes, you did," Marcos acknowledged, still scrutinizing her. "How did you come up with this?" he wanted to know. Twenty-one-year-old heiresses didn't ponder recipes and ingredients—they thought about parties and having a good time with five hundred of their "closest friends."

Wendy shrugged. The entire process had simply come to her, but she doubted if this man with the wickedly penetrating eyes would understand that. "I just did."

"You experimented at home, making trial samples?" Once the words were out he could almost envision her in a state-of-the-art kitchen, half-filled mixing bowls scattered everywhere and splotches of cream dotting various parts of her hands and face....

Marcos forced himself to erase the image from his mind because its effect on him was not what he wanted going on right now, just as he couldn't quite figure out how the heiress had actually come up with something so good that eating it almost qualified as a heavenly experience.

"No, no experimenting. At least not at home," she amended. "I just did it here. Now."

Marcos was looking at her as if he didn't believe her. Why didn't that surprise her? Well, she didn't care what he believed—she knew that she was telling the truth. As did the chef.

But for Enrique's sake—and peace—she continued explaining. "One thing seemed to go with another and before I knew it," she gestured toward several other parfait glasses on the next table, all filled with the same creamy dessert she'd just concocted, all intended for the other kitchen staff, "I came up with that."

"That," Marcos repeated, with more than a little self-deprecating defeat woven in through the wonder. Even if she had come up with it—and he wasn't completely convinced that she had—there was no denying that it was damn good. He had absolutely no doubts that the customers would love it. "Do you have a name for it yet?"

She grinned then. That grin he'd begun to think of as the visual illustration of an old-fashioned rebel yell. "I don't name my food, Marcos. Not if I'm going to eat it. Seems kind of cannibal-like, don'tcha think?"

He didn't answer her. How could he? He didn't even know where to begin with that kind of logic.

So instead, he turned to Enrique. "We're going to have to call it something if it's going to be on the menu. What do you think of Heavenly Sin?"

Enrique slanted a glance in Wendy's direction, his smile appreciative and approving. "I try to think of it as little as possible."

"As a name for the dessert," Marcos stressed, his impatience approaching critical mass.

"Oh, I see." Enrique nodded, as if rolling the name over in his mind. "It works for me."

And he was quitting while he was ahead, Marcos thought. The longer he took with the name, the more time that gave to Wendy to throw a wrench into the works, making it grind to a halt.

"Heavenly Sin it is. I'll see about having an insert placed in tonight's menu." He focused exclusively on his chef. "Do you think you can come up with several dozen of these for tonight?"

"No problem, right, Wendy?" Enrique

asked, deflecting the question to the dessert's creator.

"No problem," she echoed with confidence, her eyes shining.

"You're still taking care of the dessert," he told Enrique. They were temporarily short one dessert chef—theirs had quit last week because her husband had gotten a job in another part of the state. Marcos was still interviewing replacements. He turned his attention to Wendy. "I'm going to want you on the floor," he informed her.

He was caught completely off guard when Wendy smiled widely and said, "Why, Marcos, most men usually buy me dinner first."

It took him a second to realize what she was saying to him. And longer to get the heat that shot through him under control and compose himself.

"That's another thing," he began when he finally found his tongue. "You haven't been here long enough to call me Marcos."

And my guess is that you never will be.

"So that's, like, a milestone?" Wendy asked him.

"Something like that," he muttered. All he wanted to do right now was get away from her so that he could effectively regroup. And draw a breath without inhaling her delicate perfume.

"So when *do* I get to call you Marcos?" she asked.

There was something about the way she said his name that sent ripples through him. High, tidal wave type ripples.

He definitely didn't need this.

"When pigs fly," he muttered under his breath. Or thought he did.

It turned out that she'd heard him. "I'll be watching the skies, then," she promised.

Marcos didn't have to look—he could hear the wide grin in her voice. As he walked off, back to his office, he couldn't help wondering what he had done so wrong in his life to merit being saddled with her. He also wondered what he'd have to do in order to wipe the image of her sexy smile from his mind.

Damn, but he'd never been so happy to get the results of a lab test before, Flint thought, as he hung up the phone in his hotel room.

He'd paid extra to have the results rushed through instead of taking the customary four to six weeks. He knew he wouldn't be able to stand the tension or put up with the waiting, even though he was fairly certain that he hadn't fathered the infant causing all the fuss.

Well, part of the fuss, he amended. The rest of it surrounded his missing uncle, who was also the baby's uncle—or some such relation, he thought. Of late, the exact delineation of family dynamics were beginning to elude him.

Not that he allotted a great deal of concern to William's disappearance. Hell, plenty of men got cold feet and took off right before their wedding—or wished they had the guts. His uncle had just thought better of surrendering his freedom for a wedding band, that was all.

Uncle William would turn up eventually, relieved or sorry. But either way, the man would be alive and breathing.

Just like him, Flint thought, heading out of the hotel and out onto the street.

God, that was a relief, he thought again. He hadn't realized just how heavily all this had been weighing on him until he'd gotten the word that he was in the clear.

He might be, Flint thought, but some other male Fortune sure as hell wasn't. And it was someone close to home.

The technician who had called him had told him that while he hadn't fathered the infant, he did have certain markers in common with the baby's father. When he'd asked the technician just what that meant, the woman had explained to him that most likely a sibling of his *had* fathered the baby.

That meant either Ross or Cooper was the father, and Flint really doubted there was a chance in hell that it was Ross. His oldest brother was head over heels in love with his wife, Julie.

That left Cooper.

Cooper. His other older brother hadn't been around for a bit. Cooper had the really annoying habit of just disappearing for whole pockets of time, vanishing as if he was one of those mountain men from two hundred years ago, living off the land and keeping to himself.

Truth be told, Flint had been pretty surprised to see Cooper at the church. He thought for sure that Cooper would pass on what, by any other name, amounted to a family reunion. One that had ended badly, granted, but nonetheless had been a gathering of the various branches of the clan.

Could Cooper be the father?

It seemed to Flint like a lot of things were pointing to that, but right now he didn't feel like spending his time trying to puzzle that out.

He just felt like celebrating.

Flint got into his car and drove around, looking for some place suitable for him to celebrate his relief and joy.

When he saw Red, he decided it had to be fate. After all, his baby sister was now married to a Mendoza—Roberto—and it looked as if she was finally happy, after all these years and with one disastrous marriage behind her. That meant a lot.

Red it was, Flint thought, turning his vehicle into the parking lot. He parked the car in the first available space he could find, got out and made his way into the restaurant.

A warm wall of noise—voices weaving in and out, festive Mexican music in the background and every so often the clatter of dishes and silverware—greeted Flint as he pushed open one of the massive oak doors.

"Table for two?" the hostess at the reservation table asked him as he crossed to her.

"One," he corrected, reveling in the sound of that for the time being.

"This way, please." The young woman seated him, then handed over a menu.

He'd barely started perusing the choices when a vivacious waitress with long, slender legs that made a man's mouth water approached him with a smile that would have taken the chill out of an arctic blizzard.

"Hello, my name's Wendy, and I'll be serving you tonight," she informed him, her voice inspiring a melody in his head that he had a hunch was going to stay with him for a long, long time. The waitress leaned forward, her eyes sparkling. And just like that, she seemed to create an intimate air reserved for just the two of them. He found himself lost in admiration.

"Got your eye on something special?" Wendy asked.

Flint found himself really tempted to say, "You," but he'd just gotten out of what could have been one hell of a dilemma. He wasn't about to jump feet first into a new one.

So instead, Flint retired his menu and asked, "What would you suggest?"

"Well, now, that all depends on what you've got an appetite for," Wendy answered.

These days, Flint lived in Colorado. There was nothing fresh off the farm about him, and he knew that the waitress's friendliness just went with the territory, that she meant nothing by it.

But all that considered, he would have liked just one taste of that pretty little mouth of hers.

So, to divert himself, he glanced back at the menu, zeroed in on one of the items and said, "This steak dinner sounds pretty good." He laced his hands together, resting them on top of the menu. "I'll take the prime rib. Rare," he said before she could ask.

Wendy's smile continued as if it would never end. "Man after my own heart," she told him, making the notation. "Love a good steak myself." She looked up at him. "And what would you like to go with that? We've got baked potatoes, fries—"

Wendy continued, reciting the rest of the selections that went with the entrée he'd ordered.

Flint hardly heard a word she was saying. He was far too busy watching her lips as she gave him his options.

And he wasn't the only one.

From across the room, Marcos was doing his own observing. Just as he had for more than several days now. He told himself that it was part of his job. He was on the lookout to make sure everything was executed properly and that there were no glitches anywhere, no cause for any patron to complain about the service at Red.

It was the same reason that he took random samples of the food that came out of Red's kitchen. He had a discerning palate as well as a discriminating eye and it was up to him to keep things operating at top levels. That was what his aunt and uncle were paying him for.

However, when it came to Wendy, if he was honest with himself, he had to admit that he spent more time than he really should observing her.

Marcos could feel his temper rising as he watched Wendy leaning over this latest customer of hers, who was practically drooling over her. He frowned. Deeply.

Agitated, Marcos knew that he should just let the matter go and return to his office. After all, no harm was being done, it wasn't as if he had nothing else to do. There was payroll to review and inventory to verify before Friday came around. Fridays were when he had to place the new orders for the coming week.

He knew what he *should* do, but somehow Marcos found himself striding across the floor toward the table that Wendy was lingering over—and toward the man with the large eyes.

"Everything all right here?" he asked, struggling to sound cheerful and welcoming.

The customer looked up and nodded with an appreciative smile. "Couldn't be better, Marcos."

Marcos had actually been looking at Wendy. But now his attention was drawn to the man who had called him by his first name.

Marcos looked at him closely, then nodded to himself as recognition whispered across his brain.

"Cooper?" he asked a tad uncertainly.

"No, it's Flint." It was Wendy who corrected him. "Flint Fortune. Seems like we Fortunes just keep turning up everywhere," she said cheerfully. She tapped the tablet in her hands. "I'll go see about getting your dinner started," she told Flint, then sauntered away. Her hips moved rhythmically as she departed.

"Nice girl," Flint commented with feeling.

"So the customers tell me," was all Marcos trusted himself to say. And then he looked toward Flint. "Let me know if you need anything," he said just before he took his leave. He had a restaurant to run. And dwelling on one temporary waitress—because he refused to think of her staying on in any kind of permanent capacity—was not going to help him accomplish that.

Chapter 7

When Wendy had first come to work at Red, she'd approached her position as a waitress as if it was all just a lark. If it worked out, fine. If not, so be it.

Her parents had shipped her out to Red Rock thinking that she'd find both herself and a work ethic. When the first position at the Fortune Foundation hadn't worked out, the restaurant had suddenly become the next stop on the Wendy train to nowhere, she'd thought sarcastically.

But working at Red had turned out to be better than she'd anticipated. She'd made friends here and was even enjoying herself, something that *really* surprised her.

The one sticking point for her had been Marcos.

Funny thing about that. The harder the restaurant manager seemed to lean on her, the more she dug in. Rather than breaking, or throwing in the towel—the way she suspected he wanted her to do—she'd decided to show him that she wasn't the hopeless little trust-fund baby he obviously thought she was.

Staying on had become a matter of pride, something she'd discovered, to her surprise, that she actually had in spades.

Who knew?

So when Marcos walked into the kitchen the next morning about an hour before they opened for lunch and looked her way, Wendy braced herself to survive yet another round of parrying and thrusting. She was, she silently told herself, getting pretty good at that.

Nodding a greeting at Enrique, Marcos wasted no time, turning his attention directly to Wendy. She had annoyingly haunted his thoughts throughout last night's date with Jacinta Juárez, a woman who by all rights should have completely and exclusively dominated his every waking moment with her.

But she hadn't.

Hadn't because at the most inopportune times, thoughts of Wendy's smile or hints of that accent of hers would suddenly burst into his brain, distracting him and ruining what should have been a perfect evening with a very desirable woman. He'd wound up taking her home rather than to his bed. And it was all Wendy's fault.

"Good morning, Wendy." Marcos mouthed the greeting automatically to get it out of the way. "I want you working in the kitchen today."

This wasn't the first time he'd ordered her to stay in the kitchen rather than serve out in the dining area. Exchanging a look with Eva, Wendy suppressed a sigh.

"What am I peeling today?" she wanted to know, raising her eyes to his. "Potatoes or carrots? Or is it both?"

"It's neither," Marcos informed her tersely. He looked impatiently at the rest of the staff and they took the hint, making themselves scarce. All but Enrique, who made it his business to know everyone else's. The chef waited expectantly.

Wendy stiffened. She was confident enough in her own skin now not to want any special treatment, but neither did she want to be singled out for all the mind-numbing chores that required absolutely no skills whatsoever.

For a glimmer of a moment, as a hint of anger flitted across her face, Marcos saw his way out. But then, because right now it served his purposes better to have her stay on than to leave, Marcos let the opportunity pass. Especially since he'd sampled what she could do in the kitchen. And Enrique had assured him that Wendy was capable of more, so much more.

And, after yesterday, Marcos knew that the man had turned out to be right.

He was far too good a restaurateur to pass up a talent like hers just because she was incredibly irritating—and alluring—and had taken to haunting his dreams.

"I'd like you to take charge of desserts," he said evenly.

"Desserts?" she asked, incredulous. Her eyes narrowed as she continued looking at Marcos.

This had to be some kind of a trick.

Or a cruel joke.

At her expense.

But the next words out of the restaurant manager's mouth proved her fears wrong.

"Yes, desserts." Each word seemed to burn on his tongue as he said, "I want you to make some more of that thing you came up with yesterday."

He still didn't actually believe that Wendy was responsible for creating the confection all by herself on the spot, but this was no time to get into a discussion about it. They would be opening the restaurant doors in less than an hour and he needed to have a number of those desserts ready to go the minute an order came in for it.

"Think you can do that?" he asked pointedly.

Hot words rose in her throat as the temptation to quit nearly overcame her. But then what Marcos was saying registered.

The man was actually acknowledging that she'd done something right! It couldn't have been easy for the Marcos she'd come to know to say that, she thought.

So she smiled warmly and said, "I think I might be able to manage that for you, Marcos."

He started to tell her that she still had no right to be that familiar with him, but then he let it go. He wasn't about to continue playing games with her.

Oh, no? What do you call all but begging her to whip up her dessert so that you could list it on the menu again? Whose game is that?

Marcos pressed his lips together, suppressing yet another sigh, and did his best to ignore the annoying little voice in his head. He still had to get out the rest of this offer.

"And when we close our doors for the lunch-dinner break—" he began, pushing each word out as if it was an unwieldy, heavy rock.

And then he stopped. This was *really* hard for him to say.

She'd drawn closer to him, as if to coax out the rest of his sentence. "Yes?"

"Feel free to experiment with anything else that we can put on the menu."

Wendy gave him a pleased look. "I'll see what I can do about that." Her eyes lit up as she continued talking to him. He could almost *see* the idea forming in her head. "There's this thing I've been thinking about." And then she plunged right into the heart of what had captured her imagination. "Chocolate with raspberries and powdered sugar, with just a tiny little pinch of—"

"Don't talk," Marcos interrupted, pointing her toward the pantry. "Do."

Wendy snapped to attention and then gave him a smart two-finger salute. "Yes, *sir*," she declared.

The woman was mocking him, Marcos

thought, as he turned on his heel and walked back out of the kitchen. He deliberately avoided looking at Enrique, who was pretending to be working.

Marcos supposed he deserved that for the way he'd treated her. He hoped he wouldn't live to regret this. Any of this.

Hell, part of him already did.

But this—all of it—was for the sake of the restaurant, he reminded himself. Nothing was more important than having Red operating at maximum efficiency—not even his pride.

He'd earn back his pride—and then some—when he left Red in top condition to go on and open his own place, using everything he'd ever learned working here, he promised himself confidently.

Marcos could almost taste it and he could hardly wait for that day to come.

What else can you taste, Marcos? asked that same annoying little voice in his head.

If he didn't know better, he would have sworn that his annoying little voice had acquired a Southern twang.

Walking into his office, Marcos closed the door behind him. He switched on the radio and turned it up louder than usual. He reasoned that if it was loud enough, it would drown out the sound of her voice, as well as the little voice in his head.

At least it was worth a try.

It failed.

She kept the phone within reach at all times.

Ever since William had disappeared and one of the happiest days of her life had instantly transformed into one of the saddest, Lily Fortune was never more than a few steps away from her cell phone. Even during her morning shower, the phone was placed on the counter next to the shower door and the ringer turned up high so there was no chance that she would miss a call.

And each time it rang, her heart would leap up into her throat and a prayer would spring to her lips. And each time, when it turned out not to be William, her heart would slowly sink and the prayer would fade.

Even so, Lily absolutely refused to give up hope, refused to remain anything but optimistic that somehow, some way, someday, William would walk back into her life as abruptly as he had walked out.

The questions that surrounded his disappearance would all be answered then, but they were of secondary importance to her. What was really important was William's return—alive and well—to the family who loved him.

Worry had stolen her appetite. Nothing tasted right to her anymore. Nonetheless, Lily forced herself to have at least two meals a day because she was determined to keep up her strength. William, she sensed, was going to need her when he returned. And he would need her to be strong. She'd be no help to him if she wound up becoming a drain rather than an asset.

So, this morning after she'd allowed the cook to place before her a lone scrambled egg with a sprinkling of cheddar cheese and a single corner of wheat toast, Lily pushed the food around her plate, finally consumed it and tried to plan her day. She wanted to be at least a little productive.

William wouldn't want her to become listless and moody in his absence. He'd told her once that he fell in love with her vitality first. She didn't want him to find her a shell of the woman he loved when he finally returned.

Lily dropped her fork when her cell phone rang, nearly knocking over her orange juice in her hurry to answer.

Flipping the phone open, she pressed it to her ear.

"Hello?" she cried, suddenly breathless in her anticipation. Breathless even though she'd only stretched out her hand. "William?"

"No, Lily, it's Drew." There was a significant pause. For a dramatic effect? she wondered. And then she heard her future stepson say, "We found him."

She felt like laughing and crying at the same time. "Oh, thank God," she cried. "How is he, Drew? Is he all right? How soon can you get back?" The questions tumbled out, one after the other. She didn't even stop to draw in a breath.

When there was no immediate response, an icy chill seized her heart. "Drew? Are you still there? Talk to me. Why aren't you answering? What's wrong?" And then it came to her. Drew was trying to brace her for bad news and at the last moment, was at a loss as to how to phrase it. "Oh, my God, Drew, is he— Is William—?"

She couldn't bring herself to say the awful, damning word.

Death had taken her beloved husband Ryan from her six years ago—she'd barely survived the loss. If William was dead, it would kill her as surely as if someone had shot a bullet at point-blank range straight into her heart.

"No, he's not dead, Lily," Drew quickly reassured her. And then he stopped, obviously at a loss as to how to proceed. "But—"

The word hung there, an insurmountable mountain of steep ice between her and the man she loved. If William was alive, everything else could be dealt with. She encouraged Drew to continue, trying very hard not to be nervous.

"But what?"

She heard the man on the other end of the line take in a deep breath. "My father's alive, Lily, but he's lost his memory." She could hear the frustration in Drew's voice as he described his father's condition. "He doesn't know who he is or what happened to him. I took him to the local hospital and had a thorough workup done."

"And?" Lily coaxed.

"And the upshot is that there doesn't seem to be any evidence of a trauma to his head." The news wasn't quite as good as it sounded. "But on the other hand, those don't always show up," Drew qualified.

She wasn't going to worry about that now. First things first.

"Just bring him home, Drew. We'll handle it. We'll handle any problem. The main thing is that William's alive and that you found him. Whatever he's been through, loving care and familiar surroundings can help him negate it," she said with incredible confidence.

"Lily, I understand what you're going through, what you *have* been through and what you're hoping will happen, but you have to understand that amnesia is something that modern medicine still can't treat effectively."

She forced herself to be patient with William's son. She needed him to be direct. "Drew, what is it that you're trying to tell me?"

This was so hard for him to say. Not because he was talking to Lily, but because it was about his father. "That Dad may never remember any part of his life before that sheriff found him sleeping in the alley."

Lily refused to be brought down. William was alive and they'd found him. That was enough for her right now. "But you just said he has amnesia, right?"

"Yes, but it's not like in the movies," he warned. "Amnesia can go away in a few hours, in a few days, in a few weeks—or it doesn't have to ever go away at all." He took a breath. When he spoke, the words were intended as much for him as they were for her. "You have to be prepared for that."

She wasn't going to think about that now,

she couldn't. It would bring her down too far and she needed to remain positive.

"Just bring William home to me, Drew," she requested again. "Bring him home and we'll handle it one step at a time from there." For the moment, it was the only plan she had.

There appeared to be nothing else that Drew could do at the moment. "I can do that," he told her with a resigned sigh.

Sensing he was about to hang up, Lily spoke quickly. "And, Drew—"

"Yes?"

"Thank you," she said with feeling, trying her best not to break down and cry over the phone. "Thank you and Jeremy for finding him for me."

"You don't have to thank me, Lily. I didn't find him just for you. I—we," he amended, "found him for all of us."

"Yes, of course. I didn't mean to imply anything else," she told Drew.

Lily began praying the moment the phone went silent. The nature of the prayer had changed now that William had been found. What hadn't changed—and wouldn't—was its intensity.

And, as she prayed, her thoughts turned to her late husband, the way they often did.

There were times that she could literally *feel* Ryan's strength here. Feel his presence. Not always, but sometimes.

Like now.

She wouldn't tell anyone, not even her children, because they'd think she was crazy or had been pushed over the edge by this latest twist involving William, but there were times that she could swear Ryan was in the room with her. Supporting her. Bolstering her.

"It is all right with you, isn't it, my darling?" she whispered softly. "You do want me to marry William, I can feel it. But I need your help, Ryan. I can't do this alone. How do I bring him around? How do I make William remember us? Remember me?" she asked.

Lily could feel tears gathering in her eyes as she spoke to the man who she could no longer see.

At that moment, she thought she felt something pass over her. A feeling.

A calming presence?

She couldn't explain it, couldn't put it into words, but she was no longer agitated or worried. And suddenly, she thought she had an answer to the question she had put to her late husband.

Very slowly, a smile began to spread over Lily's generous mouth.

Chapter 8

The best laid schemes of mice and men...

The classic saying went through Marcos's brain as he walked into Red's kitchen two days later and saw that there was already someone there.

The wrong someone.

He'd come in early, hoping to find an empty kitchen. With Wendy's foray into the world of creative pastries, he recalled his own roots as a cook and had become inspired to try his hand at it again.

When he'd first targeted working in the restaurant field, he'd started out in the kitchen. It seemed only natural. Growing up, he'd been the one to do most, if not all, of the cooking at his house while his parents were busy earning a living.

Cooking had been a source of comfort to him then. The tiny kitchen in his home had been the first place that he had ever felt as if he was in control of things. He'd nurtured that feeling and eventually it became the foundation he'd used to build his life. The confidence that arose from being able to cook not just passably but well had slowly spread out to all the other facets of his life.

Cooking had been the beginning of it all, the beginning of the man he had grown up to be.

He missed being in the kitchen, missed mixing things together and coming up with an unexpected taste or texture. Missed the serenity of cooking.

Wendy's success was urging him to go back and revisit his roots.

But if his intentions had been to putter around by himself and fall back on his own devices, the moment Marcos walked into the kitchen, he was sorely disappointed.

The kitchen *was* empty. Except for Wendy.

It was only eight-thirty. What the hell was she doing here?

Suppressing an exasperated sigh, he tried his

best not to sound as irritated as he felt when he put the question to her. "What are you doing here?"

Though she was just as surprised to see him as he had been to see her, Wendy hid her reaction well.

"I could ask you the same thing," she countered, then answered his question by glibly saying, "I work here, remember?"

She turned toward the walk-in refrigerator. Marcos followed her. "Not at eight-thirty in the morning you don't. Why did you come in so early?"

Reaching the refrigerator door, she stopped and looked over her shoulder, waiting. "Actually, I came in earlier," she confessed, then opened the door and went inside.

"How much earlier?" he wanted to know.

Finding what she wanted, a large container of heavy whipping cream and what appeared to be a helping of butterscotch pudding, she took her prizes and walked out again, kicking the door shut behind her.

"Seven-thirty," she answered as she passed him.

"How did you get in?" he asked. His eyes narrowed beneath eyebrows that were drawn together in a dark, uncompromising line.

"Who gave you a key?" There was no reason for her to have one. The fact that she did meant that someone's head was going to roll.

She placed her bounty on the stainless steel work table and headed to the pantry next. "Enrique," she replied.

"Why?" Marcos wanted to know.

She turned from the pantry so abruptly, she just narrowly avoided colliding with him. He stepped aside at the last moment, trying not to notice that his pulse rate had gone up.

"Because I told him that I wanted to get an early start on making today's desserts."

She gestured at the ingredients she was slowly gathering on the table, then went to secure a bottle of brandy from the bar in the main dining area. "So I could concentrate on making something new for the menu today." And then she moved those warm chocolate eyes toward him and turned the tables. "I told you mine, now you tell me yours," she said cheerfully.

What the hell was she talking about now? "What?" Marcos asked, utterly and frustratingly confused.

So she articulated her question slowly. "What are you doing here so early, Marcos?"

He resented her putting him on the defensive—and the effect she seemed to have on him.

"I thought I'd see what I could come up with in the kitchen," he finally told her.

Wendy's stare only became more pronounced. "You cook?"

"Why does that surprise you so much?"

She shrugged in a carefree movement that made her soft peasant blouse—she'd worn her waitress uniform just in case he wanted to put her back on the floor, he noticed—slide off her slim shoulders.

Why couldn't the woman keep her clothes where they belonged, he silently demanded.

For a second, she left her blouse the way it was, though whether by choice or because she was oblivious to it wasn't clear at first. What *was* becoming progressively clearer to him was that he found the image before him exceedingly sexy. The front of her blouse continued to move teasingly in and out with each breath she took, playing hide-and-seek with cleavage he wasn't supposed to be noticing—but did.

"I didn't know I could cook," she told him honestly. "You seem to know you can, but I can't figure out why a man with your kind of looks would even begin to know the first thing about cooking."

He didn't follow her at all. "What does the way I look have to do with anything?" It was only after a beat that he realized she'd complimented him. He forced himself not to dwell on that. She probably didn't mean it the way it sounded.

"I would have thought that'd be obvious." When he said nothing, she explained her logic further. "Just that you'd have more than your share of women wanting to cook for you, that's all."

He studied her for a moment, trying to decide whether she was just laying it on thick, trying to snow him, or if she was actually serious.

The scale tipped just the slightest bit toward serious.

He concluded that she wasn't trying to flatter him, exactly, she was just saying the words out loud as they occurred to her.

"Well, I used to cook for my brothers and parents," he told her. "It was either that or live on a diet of fast food. And having me cook was cheaper—also healthier," he threw in, although back then, neither his thoughts or his brothers' had run along those lines. Marcos had just been trying to create a dinner out of whatever he found in the pantry—and doing his best to make it taste good.

If he'd failed in his attempts to make it taste at least decent, his brothers would tease him mercilessly and he'd really hated that. He'd learned to be a good cook because, very simply, he had to.

Slanting a glance in her direction, he caught Wendy grinning broadly.

"What's so funny?" he wanted to know.

Wendy pressed her lips together and began to whip the cream, drizzling powdered sugar into it at regular intervals. "Nothing."

"You're grinning from ear to ear," he pointed out impatiently.

After a beat, she gave in. No point in making him think that she was having terrible thoughts about him. "I was just picturing you, standing on a stool next to the stove, your mama's apron covering you from your neck down to your feet, frowning over something you were cooking up in a big old pot."

"For the record," he began, deciding to set her straight, "my mother's apron was folded in half and tied around my waist. And I didn't need a stool. I was this height by the time I was twelve."

"Wow," she said as her eyes skimmed over his frame quickly.

That wasn't exactly the way the kids in his class had reacted the September after his summer growth spurt. They'd called him beanpole and other, far less flattering names. It was because of their jeering that he'd made a concentrated effort to put some meat on his bones, working out like crazy every morning and night, using a set of secondhand weights he'd gotten at the pawnshop.

Eventually the weight he'd packed on was sculpted and no one called him beanpole anymore. But they did call him. Especially the girls. Mostly they were girls in his class, but sprinkled in between them were a few "older women," sophomores from the local high school. That was when he'd discovered that he could readily get by on his good looks.

It had also been possibly the most shallow time in his life, he judged now.

"You said you cooked for your brothers," Wendy said, redirecting his attention back to the present.

He raised an eyebrow. Where was she going with this? "Yeah?"

Opening the industrial-size bottle of vanilla,

she measured out an amount simply by looking and making a judgment call.

"I was just wondering how many you had. Brothers," she prompted when Marcos just continued to look at her, apparently confused.

He was still having trouble tearing his eyes away from the front of her blouse—or lack thereof. "Three," he finally answered, then filled in their names before she could ask. "Javier, Rafe and Miguel."

She liked the way the names sounded. Manly and sexy. She set aside the vanilla after capping it. "Are you the baby?"

"Miguel is. Why?" Why was she asking all these questions? What was her angle?

"No reason," she replied innocently. Picking up the whisk, she began to whip the concoction in earnest this time. "I'm the baby in my family. The baby and the black sheep," she added with just a touch of ruefulness she hadn't managed to cover.

"Why black sheep?" he asked, curious despite his silent promise to himself not to ask her any personal questions. The less he asked, the more quickly she'd work and run out of her own questions. Or at least that had been the plan until her comment piqued his curiosity.

Wendy sighed a little before answering. He

got the impression that, though she was breezy and the closest thing to a nonstop talker he ever hoped to encounter, this was apparently difficult for her to talk about.

The whisk slowed and began to travel in an anemic semicircle as she talked.

"The Atlanta Fortunes are all high achievers. The whole lot of them are power-oriented and driven. I've never known a one of them to fail at anything they set out to do—they refuse to." She stopped abruptly and looked at Marcos. He'd be right at home with her parents, she thought. "I guess you could relate to that."

He blinked, caught off guard by the observation. She did that a lot to him, he thought. Caught him off guard. "Me?"

"Yeah, you're a lot like them," she told him, leaning back a little in order to look him over from head to toe. "They'd approve of you."

The way she emphasized the last word made him wonder what she was *really* saying. It wasn't as if he wanted to get to know her and this was wedging the door open, allowing him to get a better look inside her life.

Still, there was no missing her tone, so he heard himself asking, "And you think that they don't approve of you?"

A rueful smile curved her delicate mouth.

What he really hadn't expected was his reaction to the hint of sadness. He found himself wanting to put his arms around her, to chase away that look. It didn't really suit her.

But it did make her more real.

"They never said that in so many words," Wendy admitted with a careless shrug of her shoulders, as if to make little of the matter. Her blouse slipped a little lower. He forced himself to look at her face. "But it's there, in their eyes. Oh, I know they love me," she was quick to add in case he thought she was feeling sorry for herself. She wasn't, she really wasn't. "But I've actually been a major disappointment to them for most of my life."

It really hurt her to admit it, to actually put it in so many words, but she knew that it was best for her if she got right out in front of it.

So that no one else could throw it in her face.

And then the grin was back, a little forced, but there. "That's why they've sent me out here. They keep hoping I can find something to do with my life besides just taking up space."

She reached for the canister of powdered sugar and measured out a cup, then drizzled it along the outline of the new black-and-white pudding she'd managed to create while talking to him.

"I'm the last one of six," she continued, then paused as she pressed her lips together. "Nobody's ever come right out and confirmed it, but I've got a feeling that only five of us were planned." The smile never reached her eyes. "I was the surprise they hadn't counted on."

This was a far different Wendy than the one he'd gotten accustomed to.

Maybe that was why he heard himself saying, "Sometimes a surprise turns out to be the best part."

The sigh that escaped her lips was larger this time. She quickly pulled back her lips in another grin, attempting to cover up the moment of weakness that allowed him to peek behind the mask of cheer she tried so hard to keep up.

"Maybe. But sometimes maybe not." She pushed forward the single dessert she'd been working on almost unconsciously. It was done. When he made no move to taste it, Wendy raised her head and looked up at him. She was clearly waiting for his approval. "So, what do you think?" she coaxed.

"Looks pretty enough," he allowed.

"It's got to do more than that and we both know it." She moved the dessert a little closer to Marcos on the table.

They were still very much alone in the

kitchen. No one had come in yet. The momentary silence pervaded all the corners of the wide, open room.

Somehow, as she'd lowered her guard and allowed him to look into the family dynamics she'd grown up with, she had let him see that beneath the banter and the sparkling, snapping brown eyes was a little girl who, no matter how much she said or did to deny the fact, still craved her parents' approval.

Still wanted to hear that they were finally proud of her.

In a way, Marcos could relate to that. In his estimation, anyone from a larger family could. It was hard carving out your own individuality while caught up in a group scene. Hard to be your own person and still be the daughter—or son—your parents hoped you would be.

He was fortunate enough to know that his parents were proud of the man he'd become. But if things had gone a different way…

As she pushed the plate a little closer to him on the stainless-steel surface, the spoon beside it slipped off and landed on the floor.

"Oops," Wendy murmured. The next moment she dipped down to pick up the utensil.

As did he.

Crouching down at the same time as Wendy,

Marcos found that their faces met. Her breath, soft and maddeningly enticing, seemed to whisper along his skin.

Temptation tightened his gut to the point that he had no breath of his own. The breath he drew in was hers.

The spoon—and dessert—were forgotten, as was decorum. Her eyes seemed to hypnotize him, turning him into someone he didn't recognize. Someone with longings that were being unleashed.

Marcos felt himself sliding his fingers around her face, framing it.

Wanting nothing more in life than to kiss her.

Chapter 9

What the hell do you think you're doing? Marcos upbraided himself.

He was about two seconds away from making a fatal mistake, one that would cost him.

Dearly.

He was the restaurant manager, for God's sake. Her boss. He couldn't just go around kissing the help.

But he was attracted to her.

Really, wildly, utterly attracted to her.

And he hadn't a clue what to do about it. Ordinarily, he acted on his attractions without being the slightest bit concerned.

But this situation was different and he had

to tread lightly. More accurately, he had to re-trace his steps and not tread at all.

She didn't understand it.

Why wasn't he kissing her?

To Wendy it actually felt as if time had suddenly come to a standstill. Her heart was lodged in her throat, waiting.

But the sinfully sexy restaurant manager wasn't leaning forward, wasn't kissing her. Wasn't doing *anything*.

Was he waiting for her to do something, to give him some kind of a sign that it was okay?

She'd give him a sign, all right. He might be having second thoughts about this, but she damn well wasn't.

Just as Marcos was about to drop his hands from her face, she leaned in quickly and kissed *him*. Their lips brushed lightly, like two snow-flakes falling onto one another.

One brush of lips begat another, then urged on a third. Wendy leaned further into him, taking all control out of his hands, just like that. Without thinking, without being con-scious of how he had gotten from point A to point B, Marcos instinctively deepened the kiss...until the annoying voice in his head urged him to stop.

Reluctantly he dropped his hands from Wendy's face. But needs raced so urgently through him, he caught himself gripping her shoulders as if to hold her in place even though she wasn't going anywhere.

Maybe he had done it to anchor himself. To keep himself from floating off into space, riding the crest of the wave of heat that had suddenly, wantonly materialized out of nowhere.

As if they had suddenly merged into one being, they rose to their feet together.

"You find a way to put *that* on the menu and none of our competitors will ever touch us again."

The amused voice had them leaping apart, startled, before the words were even able to fully sink in.

Now someone showed up, Marcos thought grudgingly. Why couldn't they have come five seconds earlier, before he had acted on an attraction he didn't ever want to feel?

For her part, though equally breathless, Wendy didn't look nearly as embarrassed as Marcos. In fact, she looked rather calm as she ran her hand through her hair to smooth it down.

She flashed a smile at Enrique, who was standing in the doorway, looking far more amused than a human being had the right to be in this kind of situation.

"I'm afraid there's no way I could duplicate that for a stranger's consumption," she told the chef.

Her eyes shifted to Marcos.

He hadn't a clue what she was feeling, or thinking, or even if she *was* feeling or thinking anything at all. For all he knew, this could be just standard behavior for her. After all, like the old saying went, the rich are different from you and me.

And most definitely different from him, he thought.

After a beat, Marcos realized that Enrique was saying something. He blinked. "What?"

"Do you mind if I try the dessert?" Enrique asked him again.

Unexpected anger surged through Marcos at the mere hint of what the man was suggesting, until he realized that Enrique was talking about the actual dessert, not Wendy. The pudding was still on the table where they had left it, completely untested.

He wished he could say the same about himself. But he *had* been tested just now—and had failed miserably.

It was Wendy who spoke when he didn't.

"Sure, go ahead," she urged Enrique. "I want to hear what you think of it."

Producing his own very small spoon out of his breast pocket, Enrique skimmed just the barest part off the top of the pudding, then slid the spoon into his mouth and closed his eyes. He allowed the tiny morsel to slip down his tongue and into his throat as he savored the experience almost in slow motion.

"Well, what do you think?" Wendy pressed him for a response. More than a beat of silence had passed and the chef had yet to react.

Opening his eyes, Enrique looked at the young woman he now regarded with affection as his personal protégé. Delicately, he set the spoon down.

"What I think is that this latest creation of yours is simply much too good for the masses. It should only be served to those few who are blessed with a refined, discerning palate."

"That's not how we make money," Marcos responded, finally finding his tongue. His wits, he had a feeling, were going to take him longer to locate. He had no one to blame but himself.

"A pity," Enrique conceded with a shake of his head. He looked down at the rest of the dessert, regarding it the way a man might a particularly stimulating, beautiful mistress.

"Do you have any plans for the rest of this?" he asked Wendy.

She *had* wanted Marcos to sample it, but that little detail no longer felt important, having fallen by the wayside in the wake of other circumstances. They had wound up sampling each other and discovering something far more potent than a liqueur-laced black-and-white confection.

She pressed her lips together and tasted their kiss again. Definitely better than anything she could have come up with using a dairy product, she thought.

Wendy gestured toward the dessert, indicating that the chef should have at it.

"It's all yours," she told him, then hesitated at the last moment, turning toward Marcos. "Unless you want to try it."

No, he had sampled enough exotic fare for one day. His toes were still seriously curled inside his expensive Italian leather shoes.

"That's all right, I trust Enrique's palate," Marcos said, surrendering the rest of the dessert and rubber-stamping the chef's seal of approval.

His mouth was painfully dry and his knees, Marcos realized, felt as if they were sticks of butter left out in the sun too long. Remaining where he was, he waited a second for the feeling to pass. The weakness did, the dryness didn't.

Picking up a glass, he went to the large, double stainless-steel sink and turned on the faucet. He filled his glass to the top, then downed the water.

"Put that dessert on the menu," he instructed Enrique.

"How many do you want me to have Wendy make?" Enrique addressed the question to his back.

Marcos turned around, considering his answer. They were booked solid this afternoon. Any walk-ins were going to have to stand in line and wait before they could be seated. The menu had already been set, but he wanted to lose no time in previewing this latest marvel she'd come up with.

"Start with four dozen," he decided. "If that turns out not to be enough, make more."

Enrique nodded, then realized he had one more thing to nail down before he let Marcos get away. "Do you have a name for this one?" he called after the manager. Marcos had wound up being the one to name the other dessert Wendy had produced.

Pausing, Marcos turned around again. He

looked from Enrique to Wendy, both of whom were apparently waiting for him to christen this latest miracle in a fluted glass.

Names came easily to him, but not this time. Due to circumstances beyond his control, his brain wasn't working at its maximum efficiency at the moment.

"Since this has become an ongoing thing, why don't we just have a section on the menu called Desserts by Wendy? Under it we can describe the Special of the Day." Marcos looked pointedly at the woman who had quite literally rocked his world—not an easy feat considering that he was hardly a monk and hadn't been since he had turned fifteen. "I'll leave the description up to you," he told her.

That said, he turned on his heel and walked out, quickly this time, before anyone could think of anything else to ask him. Right now what he needed most of all was a little bit of space to himself and some time to attempt to sort things out and put them in their proper perspective.

She really *had* set him on his ear.

That shouldn't have happened. He was going to have to watch himself, Marcos thought, taking careful, measured steps to his office, still feeling more than a little unstable.

Thank God it had been Enrique who had walked in on them. He trusted Enrique. Enrique knew the value of keeping his own counsel and not breathing life into rumors.

Had it been anyone else, Marcos knew that he would have had a huge problem on his hands.

Distance. He needed to maintain distance between himself and Wendy, he decided. No matter how tempting her lips were, or how much he had thoroughly enjoyed that kiss—and he had—it was something that couldn't happen again.

No one had to tell him that she would be moving on, undoubtedly soon. And he was going to be staying here. Nothing could be allowed to happen between them because it had no possible future.

Not that he wanted a future, Marcos immediately amended.

Besides, Wendy Fortune was his employee. He had to remember that. The not-quite-so-innocent kiss that had exploded between them had absolutely no place here. He was her boss, not her boyfriend, although he had to admit, if only to himself, that the latter was beginning to sound more and more appealing. But that didn't change the facts and the facts were that

they had names for a boss who forgot to behave like a professional with the woman who
worked for him. It could be seen as taking advantage of the situation—and that was the very
last thing he wanted.

Damn, but life certainly had gotten incredibly complicated, he thought humorlessly.
When had that happened?

Wendy felt like a small lifeboat that had
suddenly run aground. But obviously, she was
the only one who'd felt the earth move during that kiss. Marcos had looked like a cool
cucumber.

But then, she thought, the man did have a
reputation as a playboy. Kitchen gossip had
filled her in about that the first day she was
here.

She looked at the chef, who was busy bringing out more of the same ingredients she'd just
used to create today's prototype dessert. She
fell into step with him, lending another set of
hands to the task of carrying back the industrial-size containers.

"I think Marcos hates me."

Enrique laughed. "It did not look that way
to me from where I was standing."

Wendy shook her head. "*I* kissed *him,* Enrique, not the other way around."

"And he obviously hated every second of it," Enrique responded with amused sarcasm.

But she wasn't convinced. "I caught him off guard. Surprised him."

He tried hard not to laugh at her. He couldn't help wondering, had he ever been this young himself?

"Maybe so. But, Wendy, I know the man. He is not now, nor has he ever been, a weakling. He would have found a way to gently but firmly stop you if he had wanted to. Since he didn't, it is my professional opinion that he wanted to kiss you, too."

"In your opinion," she emphasized.

He smiled and nodded. He had no problem with that. "In my opinion," he repeated. And then he glanced at the clock. His attention was drawn back to the fluted glasses they were lining up in rows of four. "But I will not be able to vouch for his feelings if we do not have these desserts ready in time."

It didn't take a genius to understand what the chef was telling her. "So I should stop talking and work faster."

He smiled broadly, opening the first container. "Exactly."

* * *

There was only one way to deal with this, Marcos decided as he sat back in his chair. What he needed to do was something drastic in order to put Wendy off. And, in his far from limited experience, nothing put off a woman better than seeing the man she was interested in out with another woman.

He didn't know if he was being fair—or accurate—by putting Wendy in that category. She might very well *not* care about him. But the fact remained that she *had* kissed him, and that had to mean something, right?

Well, whatever it meant, he was fairly certain that if she saw him at the restaurant with a date, she would realize that he enjoyed his unfettered lifestyle and liked being in a position to see a different woman every night, if he was so inclined.

No woman liked being lumped into a group. Each thought she was special and should be treated accordingly. And while he might be willing in a moment of weakness to concede that, the way he'd remained free so far was by playing the numbers, rotating partners and always being one step ahead of a serious romance.

He was too young to settle down, he silently insisted.

He had his whole life in front of him and all the time in the world to be a good, dedicated husband if that was in the cards for him down the road. Way down the road, he emphasized. But not now. Definitely not now.

Making up his mind that having other women run interference for him was the way to go, Marcos nodded to himself, pleased.

He took a cleansing breath. No time like the present to put his plan into action.

Marcos pulled open the middle drawer in his desk. Rummaging around, he shifted several handfuls of loose papers until he located what he was looking for: his personal BlackBerry. It was an electronic version of what men had once referred to as their "little black book." Powering up the device, he began to review the names.

He was searching for just the right girl— not to turn him on, but to turn Wendy off. If he couldn't accomplish that, he had an uneasy feeling that he was going to be in trouble. Serious trouble.

A man could remain strong only for so long.

Wendy came through the kitchen's swinging double doors, making her way into the restaurant's main dining area.

The sound of high-pitched, feminine laughter seemed to rise above the usual din of blending voices. She didn't even have to look to see where it was coming from. The sound grated on her nerves.

Marcos was at it again. He'd brought another bimbo to Red.

It had been more than a week since she'd been out here, waiting tables. To her surprise, she discovered that as much as she liked creating desserts and feeling the sense of accomplishment that came from having done something new and different, she'd missed interacting with the customers.

She liked people, genuinely liked them. Liked talking to them. She enjoyed the diversity she encountered on a daily basis. The people who lived in and around Red Rock mingled in with tourists as easily as cards being shuffled at a poker table.

This, Wendy had already decided, was the year of her self-discovery.

Her parents had been right after all.

Who knew? she thought with a grin.

Her parents, now that she thought about it, seemed to be growing smarter with every year that she grew older. Also a revelation, Wendy thought, amused.

Stopping at a table with a party of four who had recently been seated, she took out her electronic pad. Greeting them brightly and asking if they'd had enough time to decide what to order, she abruptly stopped when another burst of annoying laughter rose above the din.

Doing her best not to frown, she broke down and looked in the general direction it was coming from. She wanted to see who Marcos had brought with him this time. So far, it had never been the same girl twice.

Scanning the room quickly, she thought she saw the woman responsible. And then she saw why the woman was laughing the way she was. Marcos was leaning in to nuzzle the woman's neck ever so lightly.

Wendy almost dropped the electronic pad she was holding.

One of the customers was talking to her but she only heard a faint, indistinguishable buzzing sound in her ears. It was completely drowned out by the laughter coming from Marcos's companion.

If she hadn't known better, Wendy would have said that her heart was constricting in her chest. She'd thought that kiss had meant something to him—the way it had to her.

Damn him, anyway.

Chapter 10

Technically, she shouldn't have been so surprised. After all, this wasn't the first time that Marcos had turned up at Red with a date. In the last week or so, there'd been several times now when he'd left earlier than had been his custom, only to return with some fetching, over-made-up, under-clothed eye candy draped all over his arm.

While Wendy had grown used to his mingling with the customers, seeing him squiring around a variety of women still caught her off guard.

But this time around was even worse than usual.

This was the first time that she'd seen Marcos being *really* affectionate with his date. While she knew that the restaurant manager wasn't exactly a practicing monk or celibate by any stretch of the imagination, she did think of him as someone who behaved with decorum.

More to the point, she thought of him as someone who had too much class to behave like some wet-behind-the-ears, hormones-in-a-fever-pitch adolescent.

Maybe, she thought darkly, she'd been giving Marcos too much credit.

But in the kitchen that morning when she'd kissed him, she'd seen him struggling to keep her at arm's length, or at least fighting the urges she clearly saw in his eyes.

She refused to believe that the reason he hadn't kissed her first was because he hadn't found her that attractive. He certainly hadn't kissed her back like someone who was phoning in his response.

Damn it, she *knew* he was drawn to her, attracted to her. So what was all this different-girl-every-night thing all about?

Was he trying to impress her?

No, there was no need for that. He knew he didn't have to impress her. He had to know that she liked him. So why—?

All she could think was that he wanted to make her back off.

She could think of only two reasons why a man would do something like that. He wasn't that into her, which she'd already discounted, or he was *too* into her and that scared him.

Her eyes widened as the idea registered. Marcos was into her. *Really* into her.

Wow.

"Um, miss?" The man closest to her left at the table she was presently waiting on was hesitantly trying to get her attention. "I think we're ready for those appetizers now."

Coming to, Wendy flashed him an extra-wide smile. "Yes, of course you are." She looked around at the rest of the six people seated at the table. "And just because you've all been so patient, the appetizers'll be on the house," she promised.

She had no problem making a pledge like that. The money to pay for the appetizers would be coming out of her own pocket. It was the least she could do for allowing herself to get so distracted.

Wendy glanced down at the electronic tablet she'd almost dropped, checking the notations she'd made on it. There were six different drinks listed.

"Jason will be right by with your drinks," she told them. The next moment, she turned on her heel and was heading toward Marcos's table.

He wasn't sitting in her station. She doubted if that was just an accident. Wendy nearly collided with Miranda, the waitress whose table it actually *was*. Cutting the raven-haired woman off, Wendy half turned her body toward Miranda's and said in a low voice, "I'll pay you if you let me take this one."

Miranda looked from the occupants of the table to Wendy. A knowing look came into her dark eyes. "How much?"

Wendy slipped her hand into her skirt pocket and produced a bill. "Twenty."

The other waitress plucked the bill from her fingers, happily surrendering the table.

"They're all yours, honey."

As Miranda backed away, Wendy squared her shoulders, then crossed the last few steps to the table where Marcos sat with his latest date, a petite, brassy blonde who looked as if she subsisted on less than a tablespoon of birdseed a day.

The woman, in Wendy's estimation, was seriously thin and appeared to be almost all angles. She would have pegged Marcos as the type who liked a few curves on his women. Wendy couldn't help wondering if his date was even capable of casting a shadow.

"Good evening," Wendy greeted them with a cheerfulness that was almost overwhelming. Addressing Marcos's date, she made her introduction. "My name's Wendy, and I'll be your server tonight." Looking from the woman to Marcos, she asked, "You two decided what you want? I mean, from the menu?" she deliberately clarified with a barely hidden smirk. "It's pretty clear what you want off the menu." She punctuated that with a wink aimed at Marcos's companion.

The woman looked a little offended, then smiled and deliberately slipped her hand over his on the table. It was a blatant display of territorial rights that wasn't lost on Wendy.

Marcos did his best to defuse the moment. He didn't want a scene playing out in his restaurant.

"You'll have to forgive Wendy," he said to his date. "She's got this condition that makes her say the first thing that pops into her head." Turning to Wendy, he curtly introduced his date. "This is Leila."

Closing the menu, he took the liberty of ordering for both of them. The look in his eyes as he handed the menu back to Wendy warned her to back off.

Wendy dutifully made the notations, then looked up at him. "Sure that's not too much for your lovely date?" she asked sweetly. "She doesn't look like someone accustomed to eating very much."

"Don't worry about me," Leila assured her with a smile Wendy could only describe as self-satisfied. The woman slanted a look at Marcos. "I've got a *really* big appetite."

"Lucky for Marcos," Wendy replied serenely, not rising to the bait. She retired her stylus as she continued looking at the woman. "I'll be back with your drinks before you can count to ten. *If* you can count to ten," she added under her breath.

"Are you going to let her talk to me like that?" Leila demanded, incensed.

As anger blazed in Marcos's eyes, Wendy retreated with the order.

"Are you looking to get fired?" Eva hissed at her as the other waitress followed her back to the restaurant's bar.

Wendy placed Marcos's order on the counter in front of the bartender, a physical-education student in his last year of graduate studies. For a student, he had exceptionally fast hands. The drinks were ready in a heartbeat.

"No, why?" she said to Eva.

"Don't give me that," Eva said impatiently. "You know you just can't go insulting the boss's date like that."

"Watch me," Wendy countered serenely, then, because this was Eva and Wendy really liked her, she added, "Anyone who dates a woman like that deserves what he gets."

Eva put her hand on her shoulder, silently stopping her. "Wendy, I like you. We all like you," she emphasized. "Nobody here wants to see you get fired. Trust me, that bimbo isn't worth it. Pretend it's just another table," she counseled, despairing that her advice was falling on deaf ears. "What are you doing waiting on them, anyway? That's Miranda's station."

Wendy shrugged, as if it was no big deal. "I gave her a twenty for it."

Eva pressed her lips together. Then, hunting through her pockets, she came up with three fives and five singles. She held the money out to Wendy. "Here's twenty. You're even now. Give the table back to Miranda," Eva coaxed her.

Confusion lifted as Eva's motivation dawned

on her. "You really don't want to see me get into trouble, do you?" Wendy realized out loud.

Eva refrained from uttering the all-encompassing "duh," and instead told her, "That's what I've been saying."

No one had ever really cared about her that way before. No one had ever been willing to part with their hard-earned money in order to protect her. Twenty dollars in her world meant nothing. But she knew that in Eva's world, it meant something important. It meant money for diapers and formula.

Touched, Wendy pressed the money back into Eva's hand. "Keep your money, Eva. I'll be good," she promised.

"You're already good," Eva contradicted. "I want you to behave."

Wendy laughed. "Okay, that, too." And then, as the bartender placed the two drinks on a tray before her, she held up two fingers in a solemn pledge. "Girl Scout's honor."

Eva eyed her a little skeptically. "You were a Girl Scout?"

"In my heart," Wendy assured her. "I was a Girl Scout in my heart."

Eva sighed, taking what she could get. "That'll have to do, I guess."

* * *

Wendy had absolutely every intention of honoring her promise to Eva, she really did. And, as she returned to bring the drinks and then the appetizers to Marcos's table, she struggled—and succeeded—in holding her tongue.

Her tongue remained immobile as Marcos's date became more and more glib, tossing what Wendy was sure Leila thought were witty remarks and crushing salvos at her with reckless abandon.

But when she returned to Marcos's table for a fourth time, bringing them two servings of dessert—the dessert *she* had carefully created just this morning, Wendy had had just about all she could take from Marcos's companion of the night.

The beginning of the end was when Leila wrinkled her nose after taking just the tiniest taste of the dessert that had been placed before her.

"What is this?" Leila wanted to know. She shivered in an exaggerated fashion as if she'd just been doused with a bucket of cold water.

"That's the special of the day," Marcos told her when Wendy made no response to the question. He slanted a nervous glance toward Wendy.

Maybe coming to Red with Leila was a bad idea, he thought.

Plucking the colorful napkin off her lap, Leila applied it to her tongue, rubbing hard as if to wipe away any trace of the dessert.

"Nothing special about this," she announced callously. "It tastes like soap." To underline her displeasure, Leila drained the glass of water beside her plate, as if she was trying to wash the offending taste away from her mouth.

The dessert he had consumed had been nothing short of perfection garnished with whipped cream and chocolate shavings. For a second, Marcos stared at Leila, completely mystified.

Then, suspicion crept in. Marcos decided to sample *her* serving.

When he did, his reaction was immediate and intense. His eyes darted toward Wendy. The waitress couldn't have looked more innocent than if she'd been born five minutes ago.

Like he believed that.

Why was she sabotaging her own dessert? Unless—

He dismissed the thought. She couldn't have been that brazen. *Why not? You were.*

He pushed Leila's dessert away. "You're right, it doesn't taste quite right."

He felt it best to be vague and evasive about the matter. His first allegiance and duty was to Red, to protect the restaurant's reputation at all costs. He couldn't come right out and give voice to his suspicions—that soap had actually been used instead of whipped cream.

"Bring her another," he instructed Wendy sternly. There was not so much as a hint of humor in Marcos's demeanor.

She could see by the look in his eyes that he was taking the bimbo's side against her. Fine, if that was the way he wanted to play it, he deserved the taste-bud-dead airhead.

"That's going to take a little while, Mr. Mendoza," she informed him stiffly. "I'm afraid that was the last one."

"That's okay, I didn't want dessert, anyway," Leila told Marcos. And then she smiled up at him seductively. "What do I need dessert for when I've got you? But I would like some more water to get the rest of that awful taste out of my mouth." She tilted the empty glass for his benefit.

For two cents…

Wendy banked down the hot response that

rose to her lips. Instead, she forced a frozen smile to her lips as she acquiesced.

"Of course. Right away," she promised with mocking cheerfulness.

Pausing to retrieve a clear pitcher filled to the brim with ice-cold water, Wendy headed back to their table in a flash. But just before she reached it, she suddenly tripped on a fork that had mysteriously appeared on the floor out of nowhere. Wendy managed to steady herself at the very last moment.

Even so, the incident was not without its casualties. The split-second stumble was enough to send a wave of water sailing out of the pitcher. And just like that, Leila was completely christened from head to toe with the icy water.

The woman's reaction was immediate and dramatic. Leila shrieked in abject horror and instantly jumped to her feet, her hand spread over her ample chest. "I'm all wet," she declared.

Marcos gave Wendy a dark look that told her she had just crossed the line. "I'll talk to you when I get back," he told her in a low, even voice that gave away nothing.

For appearances' sake, Wendy did try her best to attempt to dry the young woman off.

Leila refused to accept any help from a woman she was convinced had tried to first poison her and then drown her. She angrily pushed away Wendy's hand and the cloth she was holding.

"Get away from me!" she said hotly.

By now Marcos was acutely aware that everyone in the dining area was looking at them, taking this all in. Leila was making a scene. He couldn't have that.

Very politely, he put his hand under her arm and took charge. Picking up her purse, he tucked it into her other hand.

"I'll take you home, Leila. You need to get out of those wet clothes."

She stopped wailing so abruptly it was as if she was a radio being turned off. The smile that came in the tirade's wake didn't require a person with a genius IQ to decipher.

"I most certainly do," Leila agreed, her eyes already devouring him. "Let's go, Marcos," she purred, shooting a victorious look at Wendy as he led her away.

Wendy frowned as she watched them leave the main dining area. The busboy, Antonio, arrived and swiftly began to clean up the mess. He'd brought a new tablecloth to take the place of the wet one. Wendy moved to help Antonio set up a fresh table. "What could Marcos possibly see in her?" she wanted to know.

Amused, the busboy looked from the departing couple to Wendy. "I really don't think it's her mind he's interested in."

Wendy's frown deepened. "Yes, I know," she answered darkly.

"For what it's worth, I think you're a lot prettier, Wendy," the teenager told her. "If I was Mr. Mendoza and you were around, I wouldn't look at anyone else."

Wendy smiled at him. "You're very sweet." Too bad Marcos didn't think that way, she silently lamented. Bodily attraction notwithstanding, what could the man possibly see in that dreadful Leila woman? "Thank you."

Finishing up, she reminded herself that she still had tables to wait on. Time to stop speculating about Marcos's love life and get on with her own.

Turning, she saw one of her customers raise his hand and beckon her over.

As she approached him, she didn't have to paste a smile on her lips. Contemplating Leila and her new, wet-chicken look, Wendy was already smiling. Broadly.

This despite the fact that she was fairly certain that when Marcos returned he would read her the riot act, and he'd be within his right to do so. It hadn't been an accident on her part. She'd dropped the fork on the floor to begin with. She'd needed an excuse to trip the way she had.

And although the pratfall was guaranteed to get her in trouble, Wendy couldn't help thinking that it was damn well worth it.

Someone so self-centered and high-and-mighty as Marcos Mendoza's date deserved to be taken down a few pegs.

Chapter 11

He wasn't back yet.

Wendy glanced down at her watch. It was eleven-fifteen. The last of the diners had settled their checks and trickled out of the restaurant.

Marcos still hadn't returned. In all likelihood, despite telling her he'd talk to her when he got back, Marcos wasn't returning. At least, not tonight.

She couldn't help wondering if he'd put the incident in its proper perspective and had just decided to forget about it.

It was either that or, when he'd taken his fuming date home, she'd immediately peeled out of her wet clothing and he'd decided that what Leila had to offer was a lot more appealing than returning to Red and reading her the riot act.

Either way, she thought, apparently she was off the hook. At least for tonight.

Why she didn't at least feel a temporary relief about the situation was something she just wasn't going to think about right now.

If Marcos was happy fraternizing with airheads and women whose bra sizes were larger than their IQs, well then, that was his problem. Thank God her own tastes were not that shallow.

The main dining area and the patio around the fountain were eerily quiet at this hour. Cleanup had been even faster and more efficient than usual. One by one, the kitchen staff had left for the night.

Enrique, as was his custom, remained until the very end. He liked preparing a rough draft of the next day's menu after seeing what remained on hand after the doors were officially closed. Finishing his list of orders to the various suppliers—ready for placement first thing in the morning—he left it on Marcos's desk and walked out.

As he crossed into the main dining area,

he saw Wendy at the bar, slowly polishing the glossy surface.

Enrique paused. "Do you need a ride home?"

Preoccupied, she'd been rubbing the same spot on the bar for more than ten minutes now. At the sound of his voice, Wendy looked up at him blankly.

"I'm sorry, what?"

He nodded at the bar. "You look as if you are killing time. I am assuming that you are waiting for someone to pick you up, so I'm offering you a ride in their place," he explained. "It's been a long day."

Yes, it sure has been.

She demurred, shaking her head. "No, thank you. I'm not waiting for anyone. I have my car," she added.

"Then you are just interested in seeing how long it will take to rub a hole into the counter?" he guessed, amused.

Wendy looked down at the bar, then self-consciously stopped polishing, leaving the cloth where she'd found it. She might as well tell Enrique. Chances were the man already knew. He had a way of knowing everything that was going on at Red anyway.

"No. Marcos told me to stay put. That he'd

talk to me when he got back." She shrugged a shoulder. "But I guess he forgot."

At that moment, they heard the restaurant's outer door open and then closing again. Loudly.

Enrique exchanged looks with Wendy. "That is either the loudest burglar that God ever made, or it's Marcos, returning."

At that moment, as she listened to the front door slam shut, she wasn't entirely sure which option she was rooting for, Marcos or a burglar. All she knew was that her stomach was suddenly tightening like a wet piece of leather left out in the hot sun.

The lights in the kitchen were off. Heading to the only place where there was still a light on, Marcos marched into the dining room.

One quick scan of the area told him that there were only two occupants left on the premises. Which made one too many.

He crossed to them. "Good night, Enrique," Marcos said tersely.

Aware of what had happened earlier—everyone who worked at Red knew about the unscheduled "bath" Marcos's date had taken— Enrique assessed the situation before him quickly. And chose a side.

The chef looked at Wendy. "Do you want me to stay?"

Her eyes never left Marcos. The uneasiness she'd felt anticipating his return faded even as her chin went up. If the man was spoiling for a fight, she was not about to disappoint him by backing off and cowering. That wasn't the kind of stuff she was made of.

And she didn't need anyone acting as a shield or a go-between. If nothing else, these last few months she'd learned how to fight her own battles.

"No. I'll be fine," she assured him, then added, her mouth softening just for a moment, "but thanks for offering."

He gave her a slight, courtly bow. "Don't mention it."

"*Good night,* Enrique," Marcos repeated, his voice sounding more forceful this time.

"Make it short," Enrique advised Marcos as he passed the restaurant manager. "I need my dessert chef back in the kitchen and fresh in the morning."

"We'll see," was the only answer Marcos trusted himself to give the man in reply.

Wendy stood there, waiting for the tirade to begin—or the ax to fall. Either way, she wasn't about to take it quietly.

But Enrique's footfalls were the only sound heard for several beats, until they finally faded away and the outer door closed for a second time in less than five minutes.

They were alone.

"I didn't think you were coming back," Wendy finally said, unable to put up with the charged silence any longer. When he still said nothing, she couldn't resist asking, "Your 'lady friend' all nice and dry?"

His expression darkened. He'd said this a dozen ways in his head on his way back here tonight. He'd deliberately waited for Red to close, hoping he would calm down. One look at her and all those well-laid plans had evaporated.

"No thanks to you," he bit off.

This was like waiting for an explosion to go off, she thought. And if Marcos Mendoza thought he was going to intimidate her, he was about to be sorely disappointed.

Wendy spread her hands wide in a gesture of innocence. "I tripped. It was an accident."

He didn't believe that for a minute. He'd observed her these last few weeks. She wasn't the clumsy type. "Was it?"

Her chin went up again. He was eager for a confrontation, she could feel it in her bones.

Well, he was in luck because she wasn't going to back down. "Are you suggesting I did it on purpose?"

His eyes all but pinned her to the wall. "Did you?"

Wendy instantly went on the defensive. "Why would I?" she demanded.

"Leila thinks you did it because you're jealous of her." To be honest, the woman had harped on that point all the way home. It was the reason he had given up trying to calm her down and finally just left.

"She thinks?" Wendy asked, deliberately feigning surprise. "I didn't realize she was that accomplished."

Marcos watched her expression carefully as he asked, "Then you're not jealous?"

"If I was jealous," she told him between clenched teeth, "it would be of someone who was worthy of the emotion."

He seemed to look right through her before he finally asked, "Are you referring to her or me?"

There was lightning in her eyes. He'd never seen brown eyes flash like that before.

"You figure it out," she told him with a toss of her head.

The woman aroused such a wide variety of

emotions within him, it was hard for Marcos to keep from unleashing them.

Hell, for two cents—

Fisting his hands at his sides to keep from grabbing Wendy and yanking her closer to him, he threw out a challenge to her.

"Give me one good reason why I shouldn't fire you on the spot—other than my aunt and uncle backing your hiring," he qualified.

The coda he added just made her angrier. As if she would actually choose to hide behind something like that. She didn't need to use the couple as a shield. She could stand up for herself—and she did.

Going toe-to-toe with him, she declared, "Because I'm good, and you know it."

The woman thought a hell of a lot of herself. "Anyone can throw desserts together."

She *knew* he didn't believe that. "Not the kind I make." Her eyes narrowed. She'd had enough of this exchange. She didn't need this sort of verbal abuse. And she didn't need *him*. "You want to fire me for getting your flavor of the night wet? Fine. Fire me. Better yet, I quit!" she announced loudly, even though he was standing right in front of her.

Spinning on her heel, she pulled the apron from her waist and tossed it on the floor as she stormed away from Marcos. She'd taken exactly three long steps when she suddenly felt him grab her arm.

The next second he was swinging her around to face him again. *Really* face him.

But the protest on her lips was swallowed up when she found his mouth on hers.

Anger melted into pure heat and even though she'd started to shove Marcos back, she found herself threading her arms around his neck instead. The next moment she was diving head first into the kiss, her heart beating wildly. Ecstatically.

Marcos hadn't a clue as to what he was going to do until he was doing it.

This woman with the smart mouth got him so damn angry that he wanted to wrap his hands around her throat and strangle her. Just talking to her, trying to reason with her, had his blood boiling and pumping madly through every single vein in his body.

The smartest thing he could have done— for himself, if not the restaurant—was to let Wendy Fortune walk out that door and out of his life. Permanently.

But the problem was, he didn't want her to leave.

Damn it, she got him so angry, so charged

up, he couldn't think straight. Couldn't really think at all—except that he wanted her.

Wanted her more than he wanted order in his life.

The second his mouth touched hers, it was as if everything inside of him suddenly came out of the shadows and moved into the sunlight. Moved into the sunlight, absorbed it and wanted more. Wanted to be in the light, *her* light, forever.

She tasted sweeter than any of the incredible desserts she'd been so cleverly creating. And this was the kind of confection that he couldn't see himself living without.

His heart continued to race faster and faster, making him feverish and light-headed.

The more he kissed her, the more he wanted to kiss her. The more he *did* kiss her.

Until the urges within him demanded more. Demanded that things be taken to the next plateau.

This was why he had gone back to immersing himself in an endless stream of women. He was desperately trying to deny what he knew in his heart was true: that he was so attracted to Wendy he couldn't even breathe right.

Oh, damn, oh, damn, oh, damn, Wendy thought as everything inside of her scrambled to drink in what was happening. Scrambled to get more before something happened—like the last time—to cut her off.

This kiss was even more potent than the one the other morning.

She didn't know what time it was, what day it was, nothing. All she knew was that the core of her being was throbbing, wanting him, wanting to be made love to. Wanting to be joined together with this man.

Wendy had absolutely no idea where any of this would lead, and right now she didn't care. She'd never, *ever* wanted anything as much as she wanted Marcos right at this moment. She had no idea if they were good for each other, didn't care about a list of pros and cons. The white heat of desire within her just begged to be quenched.

Pressing her body closer and closer to him, she ran her hands along his face, threading her fingers through his hair. She caught her breath as she felt his hands running along her body, molding her to him.

Her heart leaped up in expectation. Any moment now—

And then, suddenly, he was pushing her back, away from him, as firmly as he'd been drawing her to him only a moment ago.

Confused, dazed, Wendy blinked, feeling as if she'd just fallen through the rabbit hole into a completely foreign land. A place where the only language spoken was completely unfamiliar.

For a second, Wendy thought she heard Marcos say something to her like, "I'm sorry," but that couldn't be right.

When he repeated it again, with more feeling and volume, she was forced to admit that she'd heard him correctly the first time.

"Sorry?" she echoed. "You're sorry? Sorry about what?"

Dropping his hands, he moved back from her, knowing that if he continued standing so close to her, he'd weaken and do exactly what he *couldn't* do.

"I shouldn't have done that," Marcos apologized quietly.

"Why?" she demanded, hot tears of exasperation and anger gathering in her throat. "It's the first thing today you *have* done right."

Frustration had put the words into her mouth as well as the sentiment that was behind them.

Damn it, Marcos couldn't be pulling back. Could he?

Was this a just a game to him? A game to see how far he could push her, then reel her back in? She wasn't some toy he could entertain himself with. *Why* was he doing this?

Exasperation tormented him. Marcos didn't understand how he could have allowed things to spiral out of control like this. He *knew* better, knew that he couldn't just allow himself to act on feelings, on stimuli.

He had more self-control than that—or *had* until Wendy had come into the picture.

What *was* it about this woman that made him behave like this? Like a man who wasn't thinking clearly?

Clearly? he silently jeered. Hell, he wasn't thinking at all.

Marcos found himself holding her by the shoulders again. Not to hold *her* at bay, but rather himself.

Taking a breath, he tried to make her understand what he couldn't quite comprehend himself.

"We work together," he began, selecting his words carefully.

"Yes, I noticed. You're the one who's usually breathing fire whenever I'm around," she added dryly. Wendy raised her eyes to his, trying desperately to figure out just what was going on in his head. "Doesn't mean we can't play together," she argued.

That was the whole point. It *did* mean that. "Yes, it does," he told her. He gestured vaguely in the air, as if to encircle the area around her. "This could be seen as sexual harassment—"

Was that what he was worried about? That she was going to sue him if things didn't turn out the way she wanted?

Maybe she could still defuse this with humor and get him to relax.

Wendy shrugged dismissively, winding her arms around his neck. "Tell you what. I'll just take my chances that you're not the kind of guy to drag the law in."

Marcos caught her by the wrists and slowly removed her arms from around his neck. It wasn't easy when every fiber of his being wanted to do just the opposite.

"Not me. You."

She looked at him, pretending to be completely shocked at his suggestion. "How about I give you my word I won't press charges?"

She was surprised when he took her seriously. "That's what you say now, but—"

"I've never broken my word."

She said it so simply and sincerely, Marcos found himself believing her. But it didn't change anything because it really wasn't a courtroom that made him leery. His concern went far, far deeper than that.

What had him really worried was his loss of control. He'd *never* lost control before. The closest he'd ever come before this moment was the first time she'd kissed him.

She undermined him in every way possible without even trying. In effect, he thought wryly, she was his kryptonite.

Pretending to discount her words, he shook his head. "It's not right," he maintained, his voice devoid of any emotion.

Wendy sighed. She knew a losing argument when she heard one. Still, she felt she had to ask, "Is this up for a vote?"

"No," he told her with a firmness he didn't feel, "it's not."

"All right then. If you're not firing me or making love with me, I guess I'm going home." She looked at him for a long moment, hoping against hope that he would change his mind at the last second.

He didn't.

Okay, home it is, she told herself. After all, a girl could only throw herself at a man so much, and then it ceased to be about anything mutual and just became tawdry and cheap.

"See you in the morning, Marcos," she told him in a voice that had no modulation to it.

Maybe, Wendy added silently as she walked out.

It was *maybe* because she wasn't all that sure she was up to seeing him tomorrow and all the other tomorrows that were to follow, with all this unresolved tension vibrating between them.

The bottom line was that she just didn't know if she was strong enough to want him as much as she did and know that she wasn't going to have him. Ever.

Chapter 12

Damn. What the hell had he been thinking?

That was just the problem, Marcos admitted to himself as he stared at the door Wendy had just walked through. He *hadn't* been thinking. Instead, he'd been reacting. More specifically, he'd been going with his gut instincts.

Up to this point, they had never failed him, but obviously there was a first time for everything because his gut instincts had failed him just now. Royally.

It wasn't entirely his fault, he supposed. There was something about Wendy Fortune that just short-circuited every logical path before him, every plan he'd ever laid out for himself. Moreover, just by existing, she had made him come close to betraying everything he'd always promised himself that he *wouldn't* do.

While he was always more than open to enjoying the company of beautiful women and having a good time with them, there were lines he had always refused to cross. He never socialized with an employee after hours and he never went below his general age group.

Wendy had made him break both rules.

She was twenty-one, for heaven's sake. His reaction to her had brought him damn close to being a cradle robber. Granted, there was only a five-year difference between them, but it was a major five years. There were times when he felt old for his age, and if she was any younger for hers, she'd be teething.

Besides, seeing Wendy after hours didn't fit into his five-year plan. He had mountains to climb, worlds to conquer and eventually his own restaurant to open. And his gut told him that that little lady, with her honeysuckle voice and huge brown eyes, was one major, sashaying distraction that would keep him from accomplishing any of it.

Until Wendy had waltzed into his life, he had thought that no woman alive could make him toss caution to the winds just for the thrill of losing himself in her. But there she was, his own personal lost and found. He felt as if he both lost himself in her and found a side of himself he hadn't known existed.

Rousing himself, Marcos shut off the lights and headed for the front door.

Those same instincts he was damning for drawing him to her told him that if he made the supreme mistake of giving in to the temptation presently rattling his cage—if he made love with Wendy—nothing would ever be the same again.

All of his precious, carefully laid-out plans and goals would wind up taking a backseat to his libido, something that had never happened before. And he couldn't afford for that to happen now.

He'd probably be better off if he fired her, Marcos thought, arming the security system and locking the front door.

Or at the very least, he should have allowed her to quit when she'd threatened to do that just now. But instead of letting her storm out, he'd grabbed her and kissed her. He laughed shortly to himself. That didn't exactly send her the right message, did it? It certainly didn't say very much for his survival instincts, Marcos thought darkly.

He'd done it for Red.

Not kissing her—that had been purely for him. But he hadn't let her quit, because her desserts were attracting more customers than the restaurant had ever had before. It was for the ultimate good of the restaurant that he had turned down her resignation. Wendy Fortune was a complete enigma: a food server who couldn't carry trays properly, but still patrons asked for her and wanted to sit at her station. And, despite having no training, formal or otherwise, she created fantastic desserts though she didn't know the names of half the ingredients.

And yet when she was finished, there was no denying that each creation was even better than the last one. Even though, at the time, it hadn't seemed remotely possible.

The woman made miracles happen.

Marcos sighed.

He was stuck with her and he was just going to have to make the most of it—and the least of *her,* he silently added. He was just going to have to police himself and make sure he walked the straight and narrow line when it came to Wendy.

Marcos wondered, as he walked back to his vehicle in the now-deserted parking lot, where he could get his hands on a good supply of saltpeter.

And then, as he got into his car, Marcos shook his head. With his luck, it probably wouldn't work. Somehow, she'd wind up having some kind of a natural repellent to the libido suppressant and, more than likely, her immunity would transfer to him whenever he found himself around her.

Okay, he was babbling now and making absolutely no sense.

Marcos turned the key in the ignition and peeled out of the lot. Time to head for home and try to get some sleep. Maybe he'd feel more up to tackling this problem in the morning.

But somehow, he doubted it.

This couldn't go on indefinitely, Wendy told herself two days later. Rather than being less aware of Marcos, the way she'd promised herself she would be after that fiasco in his office, now she was even more aware of him, of his comings and goings, than ever.

For whatever reason, he'd decided to revert back to his old habits, remaining at the restaurant, working, instead of clocking out early, only to return with his latest fling draped like Velcro on his arm.

At least she didn't have to deal with that, Wendy thought.

But she did have to deal with knowing that at any second she could run into him. That was when everything would turn awkward. *He* made her feel awkward, something that normally didn't happen.

This just *couldn't* continue, she thought again as she rummaged around in the store-room, looking for a sack of powdered sugar.

And there it was, she saw, right in front of her. This "thing" with Marcos was making her blind as well as crazy. First chance she got, she promised herself as she hefted the huge bag, she was going to talk to Marcos and have it out with him.

She suppressed a grunt as she shifted the load, trying to find a comfortable way to trans-port it back to the kitchen. Struggling, she made the best of it, tottering slightly as she emerged from the depths of the storeroom and turned a corner.

The next second, she was swallowing a shriek of surprise—and dropping the sack to the floor. She'd come within a hair's breadth of colliding with Marcos.

"I'm not that scary," he protested gruffly, squatting down to pick up the sugar.

Unfortunately, Wendy had automatically done the same thing, with predictable results. Their heads met and bumped—hard.

The impact caused her to lose her balance. The next thing she knew, she was falling backward.

Biting off a curse, Marcos made a grab for her arm, missed and wound up smack on top of the woman he'd been doing his damnedest to avoid.

Had this occurred with any other employee, he would have instantly jumped to his feet as if his legs were made of steel springs.

But he wasn't on top of Antonio, the busboy. He was on top of Wendy, the dangerously desirable pastry goddess. On top of her in a semidark storeroom. With no one else anywhere in the immediate vicinity and no indication that anyone would be sharing the space with them anytime soon.

His body instantly sizzled and he could literally *feel* the heat radiating from her—or was that *his* body heating up like some out-of-control furnace?

Either way, there was heat, a great deal of overwhelming heat. And such an urgent pull in the center of his core that he found it impossible to ignore and almost as impossible to resist. Especially since *she* wasn't offering a word of protest.

Heaven help him, he felt her breath along his neck, melting away what shreds of resistance he was vainly attempting to gather.

With his last ounce of self-control, Marcos put his hands down flat on either side of Wendy. He had every intention of pushing himself up off her and to his feet. But the look in her eyes froze him in place just long enough to hear her utter a single, soft word.

"Don't," Wendy whispered.

He didn't.

Instead of pushing himself up, he remained exactly where he was and found himself gathering her to him. The very hands that were going to save him had betrayed him instead.

His mouth came down on hers.

The sound of intense pleasure that escaped her lips made his blood rush and sealed his fate at the very same time.

He kissed her over and over again, his lips traveling over her face, her throat, moving down to her collarbone. Breathing hard, Wendy arched into him. An urgency prompted her to begin working his shirt buttons free.

A desperation seized him and he could feel that it was mutual. They both wanted to capture this moment before it was gone or something caused it to shatter.

The same urgency that prompted her vibrated through him. Marcos tugged the edges of her blouse out of her waistband. He slipped his hands beneath the fabric, touching her, caressing her. Wanting to possess her and make her his in every way possible.

The sound of the door closing in the distance, followed by footfalls, had both of them jerking apart and then freezing in place.

Listening.

The sound grew closer.

As if sharing one single thought, they instantly reversed their actions. Clothes about to be torn away were immediately tucked and smoothed back into place.

Gaining his feet, Marcos grabbed her hand and pulled her up.

They had time for one deep breath before their duo became a trio.

Enrique came around the corner, then stopped dead.

The chef looked less surprised to see them than they were to see him.

"Am I interrupting something?" he asked

casually, then added a single word as amusement curved his mouth. "Again?"

Wendy found her tongue first. "I was having trouble carrying this huge sack of powdered sugar," she told the chef, gesturing at the bag that was on its side on the floor where she had dropped it. "I asked Marcos if he'd help carry it into the kitchen for me."

Enrique looked impressed. "How kind of you, Marcos. I would have expected you to tell the busboy to do something so menial."

"There are no menial tasks, Enrique," Marcos replied, bending down to lift up the fallen sack. "Only menial people. We're all in Red together," he added.

Enrique, the corners of his mouth still curved in amusement, nodded his head in agreement. "Which is why Red is such a success. I am wondering, though, if you are helping her by carrying the sack." He paused significantly.

"Yes?" Marcos asked.

"What is it still doing on the floor?" There was humor in his dark eyes as he waited for an answer.

Again, it was Wendy who answered. Marcos got the feeling that coming up with instant answers and alibis was second nature to her. Undoubtedly something she'd honed as a teen whenever she was caught sneaking back into the house by a caring parent. He'd heard via the grapevine that wealth had not caused her parents to abdicate their parental authority.

"You startled us," she told the chef. "He dropped it."

"I see." Enrique smiled broadly. "Well, I came in to get the first rack of spareribs. Would you like to get those for me?" he asked, waiting for Marcos to answer. "I'm experimenting with a new sauce."

"You look strong enough to get your own rack of spareribs, Enrique." With that, Marcos hoisted the sugar to his shoulder and began walking toward the storeroom's outer door.

Wendy followed closely behind him, acutely aware that the chef was watching her every step.

Had Enrique been just several minutes later, there would have been no way that she and Marcos could have quickly resurrected decorum. Marcos would have been making love with her, and Enrique would have been there to witness it.

While the thought of an observer to this, the most intimate of acts, brought more than its share of color to her cheeks, the fact was not lost on her that, because of Enrique's unfortunate, poorly timed entrance, another opportunity had slipped through her fingers and fallen by the wayside.

It made Wendy ache inside.

Coming out of the storeroom and into the kitchen, she looked around, trying to find the man who most definitely lit her fire every time she came within tasting range of him.

The sack of powdered sugar was lying on the stainless-steel table where he had obviously put it down, but Marcos was nowhere to be seen.

Squaring her shoulders, Wendy went to see if he'd retreated to his office. On the way there, she stayed alert in case Marcos had detoured somewhere or something else had caught his attention.

But he wasn't in his office.

Exhaling a huge sigh, Wendy turned on her heel, determined to find him. They needed to have this out.

Where the hell *was* he? she wondered impatiently. Red hadn't opened for business yet. There was no way that Marcos would have already left for the day.

As she turned, Wendy came perilously close to walking into the object of her manhunt for the second time today. But this time, just before they collided, Marcos took a pronounced step back away from her.

She couldn't have put it into words exactly, but seeing him back away like that, as if she were a poisonous snake, really stung. Still, she forced herself to rally and forged ahead. They *needed* to clear the air, to get this out in the open and decide on a course of action that was acceptable to both of them.

She already knew which way she was leaning. Mentally she crossed her fingers that, despite what he was saying, Marcos was leaning that way, as well. She was certain in her heart that the man who had kissed her in the storeroom wanted her, but verbally he was throwing up so many roadblocks that he was completely confusing her.

Before Marcos could say anything to her, she announced, "We need to talk."

He looked at her and every instinct he had for self-preservation lit up like a huge red flare and a single word screamed through his brain: *Mayday!* The same message rumbled through his system.

Marcos knew trouble when he saw it and this woman was trouble with a capital *T*. He had a feeling that she always had been, which was undoubtedly why her family had sent her here to Texas.

"No," he told her firmly, "we don't." And with that, he circumvented her, walked into his office and closed the door.

His mistake was in not locking the door once he'd closed it. He hadn't even reached his desk, located only a few feet away, before the door flew open and she was right there in the office beside him.

And then, just like that, she was in front of him. In his face.

"Yes," she insisted firmly, "we do."

His eyes were dark, cautioning her to drop this subject that had no future.

"What we *have* to do is get ready to open in half an hour. If you have a special dessert to offer for today's menu, I suggest you get to it. *Now,*" he underscored. "Because if you don't have anything ready—and approved—by the time we're ready to open our doors, that space on the menu remains empty for the day." He issued his ultimatum. "The choice is yours."

She looked at him, her mouth filled with words begging to be released.

But arguing with him here and now would lead nowhere and she knew it.

And besides, he was right, she did have to

get something ready for today's menu. She wasn't about to shirk her duty or drop the ball, but neither was she going to allow herself to get distracted from having it out with him. She was just going to have to pick another time.

Pressing her lips tighter to keep from saying something that might lead to yet another dead-end discussion, Wendy nodded.

"All right, I'll get right on it," she promised.

And silently, she made him another promise, one she intended to keep.

But we are going to have this out, one way or another. You're going to have to face me—and yourself. Soon, she added with feeling as she walked out.

Very, very soon.

Chapter 13

It wound up being one of those days that felt as if it was never going to end.

Today Wendy had come up with not just one new dessert but two. She did it not because she was an overachiever, but because she felt that if she did, it would show Marcos that she was dedicated. That she took her job just as seriously as she took the thought of the two of them finally and, in her estimation inevitably, coming together.

But had Marcos said anything to her when she'd managed to top her lunch creation with the one that she offered for dinner? No, he hadn't.

It was like working for a sphinx. Except for the fact that he *did* talk to the rest of the staff as well as the patrons.

It was just her he ignored.

Enrique had been generous with his accolades, raving about the new taste sensation she seemed to have uncovered, bringing together ingredients that had heretofore not been thought of in the same context. She'd mixed together a smattering of pomegranate seeds with fresh ginger, lemon curd, cream cheese and drizzled chocolate sprinkles over the mixture as it sat atop tiny phyllo dough shells. The man actually had seconds, something he rarely, if ever, did.

At any other time, she would have been more than flattered.

But it wasn't Enrique's approval she was interested in, even though she had accepted it politely, forcing a pleased smile to her lips. All the while she had done her best not to let anyone see just how much Marcos Mendoza's silence bothered her.

She'd thought, with Enrique having a difficult time keeping the kitchen staff from sneaking off with samples of her dessert, Marcos would have said *something* that even remotely sounded like a compliment. But when she'd presented him with a serving, he'd barely tasted it, just nodding his head and muttering something that sounded like, "It'll do," before walking out of the kitchen to take an incoming call.

Probably from his newest bimbo of the day—or night, Wendy thought darkly.

She had been so angry that she could have scratched his eyes out. But that would have shown him that she cared, that he'd affected her, and she'd be damned if she would give him the satisfaction. So when he left without saying an actual, audible word, she'd pretended not to notice and made herself busy with something else.

That had been right before Eva had suddenly turned very pale and became rather unsteady on her feet. Forcing the senior waitress to sit down, Wendy had offered to take over her tables for the day, or at least until Eva began feeling better.

For the next hour or so, Wendy had divided herself between taking orders in the dining area, and the kitchen, where she prepared the desserts to fill the incoming orders. Mercifully, her dual life came to an abrupt end when María Mendoza stopped by to get an early lunch. Seeing Eva's pallor, the woman had whipped up something involving a heavy dose of ginger and bubbles and stood over Eva until she had drunk it down to the very last drop. At which point Eva shivered. A lot.

And then, just like that, the ginger-and-bubbles concoction had soothed Eva's queasy, rebellious stomach. Only then did Mrs. Mendoza indulge herself and accept the serving of Wendy's dessert that Enrique offered her. Two bites into it, she made a comment about having died and gone to heaven.

Seeking her out, the restaurant owner's wife had raved about Wendy's dessert for a good five minutes—longer than it had taken her to consume it.

Wendy *knew* that Marcos had heard his aunt, but he'd made absolutely no comment. Again he'd cocooned himself in a blanket of silence like some damn noncommunicative robot.

That's what he was, she decided heatedly. A robot. He had to be. Only a robot wouldn't have melted in the heat that had been created between the two of them in the storeroom this morning. And only a robot would have walked away without so much as a second glance because he'd so completely divorced himself from the situation.

Muttering a few choice words under her

breath about pig-headed, stubborn jackasses, Wendy walked into the women's locker room. As the door closed behind her, leaving her isolated and all alone, she made up her mind.

She was going to have to stop beating her head against the wall. Stop filling that same head with endless questions about Marcos.

She was going to have to stop *thinking* about him, period, Wendy upbraided herself. There were a lot more men in the world, better-looking men, more interesting men and a hell of a lot friendlier men than this walking enigma who was her ill-tempered boss.

The sooner she stopped concentrating exclusively on Marcos, the faster she was going to get over this. Whatever *this* was.

Desperate to leave, she ran through her locker combination. She needed to open the stationery-store lock mounted on her locker in order to get at her civilian clothes.

Just as the last tumbler clicked into place, she heard her cell phone ringing inside the narrow storage space. The call was on its third insistent ring by the time she got to her cell.

Exasperated, Wendy opened it and pressed it against her ear without bothering to look at the caller ID first. "Hello?"

"So how's it going, Wendy-bird?"

Even if she hadn't recognized the deep, jovial baritone that vibrated against her ear, she would have known who was calling. Only one person called her by the name uttered by one of Peter Pan's Lost Boys, just before Tinker Bell convinced him to shoot down a flying Wendy.

"Blake," she cried as mixed feelings stormed through her. She hadn't heard from her brother in ages, not since Christmas, when they'd all gathered at the house where they'd grown up. "Is anything wrong?"

"Ah, you still know who I am. Good." Pleasure filled his voice. "I haven't heard from you in so long, I thought maybe you forgot all about me and the others."

The phone worked two ways, she thought. But there was an even more salient point to drive home. "*I'm* not the one who shipped *you* out," she pointed out.

"Neither am I," he reminded her. "You know Mom and Dad just did it because they were concerned about you."

Because there were only six years separating them, she was closer to Blake than she was to her other siblings. They had a shorthand all their own. But it still took a second for her to realize that Blake had used the past tense when making a reference to their parents.

"They're not concerned anymore?" she asked, afraid she was misinterpreting his meaning.

She wasn't.

"Not since María Mendoza called to tell Mom what a great job Marcos said you were doing." He paused, then asked, "Marcos, that's the restaurant manager, right?"

"Right," she muttered, hardly hearing the last question as she tried to absorb what Blake had just told her. It was safer just to have him repeat it in case she *had* gotten it wrong. "Run that by me again?"

"What, hearing a compliment once isn't enough for you?" he teased.

That wasn't it at all. "Mrs. Mendoza talked to Mom?" It was something she hadn't considered.

"Yeah." She could almost hear the grin in his voice—or maybe it was a smirk. There were times with Blake that she couldn't know for sure. "You know, it's this universal thing all mothers have got going on. Keeping tabs on each other's kids."

Wendy could have sworn that her brain was moving in slow motion, the words her brother was saying bouncing off her head as if her skull was made of trampoline material.

Finally, Blake's words sank in and registered. "And she said that her nephew said I was doing a good job?" Why the hell hadn't anyone—meaning Marcos—told her this?

"The exact words Mom used was that the woman told her this Marcos guy was raving about how creative you were, and how business has actually gotten even better since you started making these fancy little mouthwatering desserts of yours. Just how long have you been able to do that?" Blake wanted to know.

Wendy shrugged in response even though her brother couldn't see her. "It's just something that seemed to come to me."

"Well, make sure it keeps on coming because I've never seen Mom and Dad happier with you. Both of them are *really* relieved that you're not going to turn into one of those self-centered, entitled heiresses."

The image stung. Granted, she hadn't exactly been an eager beaver before this, but that was because she'd thought her lot in life was to marry Channing and live happily ever after. Surprise.

"Mom and Dad actually thought I was going to become like that?" she asked in disbelief. "How could they?"

"Hey, nobody ever starts out thinking that

their kid is going to wind up wasting their life and amounting to nothing, but I can tell you that they had some real moments of uneasiness when you dropped out of college, and then again when you messed up at Uncle Ryan's foundation."

She supposed, as she listened, that she hadn't exactly done anything to reassure her parents that she would amount to something, the way they all had.

"But now they're smiling again," Blake was saying, "and you're their little golden child, just like you were when you were little."

Yeah, right. Blake was clearly rewriting history. "Oh, please. I was an afterthought."

For a second, there was silence on the other end, as if her brother was trying to untangle the meaning behind her words. And then he said, "That's not the way I remember it. You were their little princess. Later, when you messed up and then dropped out of college, both of them were afraid that they'd spoiled you to the point of no return."

This was all news to her. Had she been that wrong? Had she actually remembered things out of their proper perspective? She'd explore that later. Right now she was more interested in something else her brother had said. "And

Mrs. Mendoza actually told Mom that Marcos told her I was going a great job?"

"Yes," he replied patiently. "How many different ways would you like me to say it?"

She knew Blake probably thought she was milking this, so she explained why she was finding all this so incredulous. "It's just that Marcos never said anything to me."

"Maybe he's afraid you'll get a swelled head," Blake speculated, then laughed. "Been known to happen."

Suddenly, Wendy didn't feel exhausted and drained anymore. Instead, she felt energized. "Thanks for calling and letting me know— about Mom and Dad," she added as an afterthought. After all, her brother hadn't called to discuss Marcos with her.

"I just thought you'd be glad to know that the folks are proud of you." And then he said with another laugh, "Sure took you long enough."

She took no offense. Blake could always tease her without hurting her feelings. "It's just more dramatic that way," she replied.

All the while, her mind was elsewhere.

Why hadn't Marcos told her that he was happy with her work? Why hadn't he thrown even one decent word her way, instead of making her feel so inadequate?

"So the next time that we're both in the same city," Blake was saying, "do I get to sample one of these heavenly creations of yours?"

"All depends if you play your cards right, big brother," she countered.

Blake fell back on his standard, years-old threat. "Hey, remember, I've got those naked picture of you in the bathtub—with those dissolving bubbles."

"I was two, Blake," she reminded him.

Blake sighed. "Can't blame a guy for trying. Take care of yourself, Wendy-bird. You done good."

She thought she detected a hint of pride in his voice, as well. It made her happy. She hadn't thought that it would matter, having her brother proud of her, but it did.

"I'll talk to you soon," she promised as she terminated the call.

The moment she snapped the phone shut, her face clouded over. All this time, she'd been trying to get a positive response from Marcos. Except for that first time, when he'd assumed that Enrique had created the dessert, she hadn't had so much as a hint that he even remotely *liked* her desserts, although everyone else did, including Enrique.

It wasn't everyone else she was trying to please. It was Marcos.

Wendy changed quickly, shedding her uniform and slipping on a slim, thigh-high navy-blue skirt, a fitted, light gray sweater and her beloved four-inch strappy heels. She'd always gone for style rather than comfort.

Running her hand through her hair, Wendy took a quick survey of herself in the mirror she had taped to the inside of her locker door.

Satisfied with what she saw, she closed the door again and spun the dial on the lock to secure it.

With a determined look, Wendy walked out of the locker room.

Wendy Fortune was loaded for bear. A bear named Marcos Mendoza.

To avoid the temptation of "accidentally" running into Wendy, Marcos had left the restaurant and gone home half an hour earlier. He'd left the task of locking up to Enrique. It wasn't as if he was putting the man out. The chef usually stayed behind a lot longer than the rest of the staff.

Marcos thought darkly if he couldn't conquer his temptation, he could at least avoid it a while longer.

Rather than his getting used to having Wendy around, those insistent urges that kept badgering him were getting worse with each passing day. He actually found himself wanting the woman at completely improbable times. Found himself trying to purge thoughts of her from his head when they popped up out of nowhere.

And if that wasn't bad enough, no matter how much control he exercised over himself during his waking hours, he had absolutely no control over his thoughts when he was asleep. Which was why he caught himself dreaming about her every night. Sometimes more than once a night.

It was getting to the point that he was afraid to go to bed and close his eyes.

Afraid that his mind would betray him.

The dreams were getting sexier, more complicated and, when he woke up, usually in a puddle of sweat, all he could think of was recreating those dreams and turning them into reality.

He couldn't go on like this.

But he couldn't fire her, either, he thought. He had no basis to let her go. Dreaming about an employee was *not* a reason for terminating her. It sure as hell wasn't something that would stand up in any court.

Besides, because of Wendy, business, which had never been bad, was growing more and more phenomenal. He had no reason to let her go, no excuse he could even try to inflate and offer to his aunt or uncle. Especially after he had told his aunt, in a moment of weakness, how wonderful Wendy's desserts were.

He supposed that if anyone was to leave Red, it should be him.

But he wasn't ready to go, either. His wings weren't strong enough for him to attempt to fly solo yet. That meant that the only thing left for him was to just suck it up and somehow continue to forge on. Pretending that just having Wendy Fortune around wasn't steadily melting away his inner core.

How much could a man endure before he cracked? Or gave in?

Marcos sighed and dragged his hand impatiently through his thick, tangled black hair. He was sitting on the sofa. There was some inane classic movie on one of the cable channels flickering on the giant flat-screen before him. If his life depended on it, he couldn't have identified the name of the movie or what the story was about.

He'd been hoping that the TV would either lull him to sleep or bore him into that state, but it just wasn't happening. His brain was too wired to check out.

Possibly ever.

Another impatient sigh escaped. There just didn't seem to be a solution to this.

And then a thought hit him like some winged angel of mercy.

Maybe he was making a mountain out of a molehill, Marcos reasoned. Maybe, if they slept together, all this heightened anticipation that was ripping through him would disintegrate like so much sawdust in the wake of his colossal disappointment.

After all, he sincerely doubted that anything or anyone could live up to the expectations he had attached to the chemistry that was snapping and crackling between Wendy and him. Intentionally or not, he'd given the thought of making love with her far too great a build-up in his mind.

And he knew where that path, where having his hopes raised, always led, whether it involved being ten and hoping for something expensive and wondrous underneath the Christmas tree, or the first time he'd made love. It had been a pleasant enough experience, but the ground hadn't moved. Fireworks hadn't gone off.

It would be the same, making love with Wendy. He'd be disappointed in the end, pure and simple.

Maybe, since she seemed to be as interested as he was in making the experience happen, he should stop over-thinking all this and just do it.

And once they had this powder keg they were sitting on finally defused, it would cease to be the elephant in the room, and they could go on with their lives.

And maybe, just maybe, he'd finally get a decent night's sleep.

It was worth a shot.

Debating with himself for a moment, Marcos stared at the landline. Should he pick it up and call her?

Hell, *do it,* his brain urged.

Taking a breath, he tried to piece together what he was going to say once she *did* pick up the phone. Nerves danced through him with spiky cleats. Marcos offered up what could have passed for a small prayer and reached for the receiver.

He had no sooner started pressing the buttons on the keypad than his doorbell rang.

Chapter 14

Marcos wasn't expecting anyone at this hour. He thought of just ignoring the doorbell, but there was no point in pretending not to be home. Whoever was standing on his doorstep could see that there were lights on inside.

And if the incessant ringing was any indication, they were not about to politely take a hint and go away.

Muttering a choice curse under his breath, Marcos switched off the TV and stormed over to the front door. He yanked it open, but the less than inviting words on his lips faded the moment he saw who was leaning on his doorbell.

Wendy.

A very annoyed, angry-looking Wendy. Thoughts of bedding her and getting past the unrelenting urges that were giving him so much grief were temporarily shoved to the background.

What was she doing here at this hour? And how did she even know where he lived?

Shaking off his temporary stupor, Marcos said, "I was just thinking about you. Of course, you weren't scowling like that at the time." He couldn't come up with an actual reason for her being here, but he took a guess. "Something wrong at the restaurant?"

All the way over from Red, Wendy had been practicing her conversation with Marcos in her head, repeating passages over and over again in order not to forget them. So when he finally opened the door and was standing in front of her, she shouted the first words that rose to her tongue. Unfortunately, she wasn't starting at the beginning.

"Why didn't you ever say anything?" she wanted to know.

Marcos stared at her, more than just a little confused. What the hell was she talking about? "I wasn't aware that I was particularly mute around you."

Since Marcos wasn't inviting her in, she

took it upon herself to move the man aside and storm into his house. His flippant answer only served to annoy her more. "You know what I mean."

Turning, he closed the door behind Wendy. Damn, but that trite cliché really did apply here, he thought. His dessert wizard looked magnificent when she was angry. Her eyes were flashing and her cheeks were flushed. And all he could think of was that he wanted her.

"You're giving me too much credit," he told her. "I really haven't got the slightest idea what you mean." And that was true at least half the time, he thought.

Wendy spun around, glaring at him, her hands fisting at her waist. "You *like* my desserts."

Was that what this was about? He still didn't see what the problem was.

"Well, yeah," Marcos responded. From where he was standing, that was a given. But how did that tie in with all the fury he saw in her face? He wished she'd calm down a little because the color that had come into her cheeks as she stormed in was really turning him on—as if he really needed that extra push.

"They wouldn't be on the menu every day if I didn't."

She tossed her hair over her shoulder, still glaring at him. "So why didn't you tell me?" she demanded.

He walked back into the living room. Wendy followed him step for step like a heat-seeking missile.

"Because I thought you were bright enough to figure that out on your own," he told her. "You didn't strike me as the kind of needy person who had to have her ego stroked." He'd finally come around, seeing her as something more than just a spoiled little rich girl. Had he made a mistake? Was his initial assessment of her right after all?

Wendy blew out a breath and then pressed her lips together. He just didn't understand, did he?

"It's not a matter of ego," she finally said, throwing up her hands. "It's a matter of knowing you approve. Of one person reaching out to another and saying something nice for a change."

So she really was insecure. That was something that would have never occurred to him. "And my approval means that much to you?" he asked incredulously.

When he said it that way, it made her sound much too needy. Wendy sighed as she dragged her hand through her hair. She shouldn't have come here. This was coming out all wrong.

"Never mind," she said, a mixture of anger and resignation in her voice. Turning, she started heading for the front door to let herself out.

Stunned by her actions for the second time in five minutes, Marcos caught her arm before she could get past him and out the door.

Looking down at his hand, Wendy tried to pull away. He tightened his grip just enough to hold her in place. "What are you doing?" she demanded.

"This is me, reaching out," he said, his tone as mild as hers was sharp. "Isn't that what you just said you wanted?"

She pulled again. He continued holding her arm. "Now you're just making fun of me."

"The thought never crossed my mind," he told her with a straight face. "Other thoughts, tormenting thoughts, provocative thoughts, *they* crossed my mind, but none about making fun of you." His eyes on hers, he released her arm. "So, you never answered me. Is my approval that important to you?"

She would have wanted to deny it, to toss

her head and just keep walking, but it was too late for that. She'd already given herself away.

Hedging, she answered his question with a question. "What do you think?" The simple answer was that his approval meant a great deal to her because she cared about him—and wanted him to care about her.

Maybe he was crazy, but right now he felt that a little soul-baring truth might be in order, and might even help to clear the air.

"I think that since the day you walked into Red, my uncle and aunt on either side of you like some kind of an honor guard, I've had absolutely no peace of mind. You've tormented me every single day."

Was he referring to something she was unwittingly doing at work? Was this the beginning of yet another complaint? One step forward, two steps back, she thought, resigned.

"No I haven't," she protested.

A smile curved his mouth. A small, unfathomable, impossibly sexy smile. Wendy felt her gut tightening.

"You have no idea," he said to her softly.

All the protests that were rising to her lips died and, just like that, the room became incredibly quiet. As her pulse quickened, she swore she could literally hear her heart pounding.

Could he?

"Then show me," she coaxed in a quiet whisper.

Very slowly, as his eyes held her prisoner, Marcos brought his hands up to her shoulders, bracketing her and ever so gently holding her in place.

"You sure you want me to?" he asked. Because once he started, there would be no turning back. They both knew that.

Excitement was wrapped around the tension, shimmering in the air.

"Yes," she said, her voice so low it was barely audible. "Oh yes."

A smile came to his lips and drifted into his eyes and then, the next moment, his lips touched hers. Softly, gently, and so very lethally she was surprised that she didn't burst into flame right then and there in front of him.

The kiss deepened, ignited the rest of her body, spreading heat from her toes to her fingertips and up to the roots of her hair.

Wendy's head was spinning—or was that the room? All that was clear was that nothing was clear—except that this time, this time, her soul whispered, there would be no stopping, no interruptions from the outside world wedging them apart.

No hesitation.

No place to hide.

In her heart she *knew* Marcos wouldn't be pulling back, wouldn't be leaving her high and dry—and unfulfilled—because he wanted this as much as she did. She could taste it on his lips, feel it on his breath. Every part of him wanted her as much as she wanted him.

She felt as if there was a cry of joyous celebration echoing in her body.

And then an urgency seized her, pushing for her to step up what she was doing, just in case there *was* some sort of interruption hovering in the wings, ready to pounce, to separate them before—

Before—

She kissed him hard, transmitting her sense of urgency to him.

It was like trying to hold on to a ball of fire, Marcos thought—completely impossible without seriously singeing his hands. He'd never been in this position before, never had a woman behave like this before.

Her lips traveled along his face, his eyes,

his throat, reducing him to a swirl of heat and urges. He'd never before experienced a reaction like this to a woman. Never had a woman in his arms who made him feel this wanton, this hungry. He'd had his fair share of women. More than the average man, fewer than a card-carrying womanizer. But this was all new to him.

There'd always been a decorum, even in the wildest of frenzied moments. He'd never lost control, never lost his train of thought. Never fallen, head over heels, into an abyss.

But it was as if everything was short-circuiting now. There was only this pulsating demand beating through him, urging him to move quickly, before the moment, the opportunity, was gone. Making him feel as if he would die if that happened.

He was breathless almost from the very start though he prided himself on both his stamina and his endurance. She'd managed to steal both from him in less than a split second.

Wendy felt his hands tugging away her clothes, making urgent love to her body with each caress, as barrier after barrier disappeared.

His hands were hot. Her body was hotter.

His mouth devoured her and she returned

the favor in kind. It wasn't a sense of competition that drove her on. It was need. A need to touch, to taste, to feel and to show. She wanted him to know how much she desired him. How much he was affecting her. There was no holding back for later because there might not be a later. All she had was now and *now* would have to be enough.

More than enough.

She had no idea where any of these responses were coming from. It was as if she was channeling another Wendy, who was living through her body, making things happen, using her as an instrument.

Channing Hurston, the fiancé-who-wasn't, had been her first lover. And, until this moment, he'd been her only lover. *Adequate, but tepid* was the best phrase she could use to describe what had gone on beneath their sheets. There'd been heat, but no fire. A satisfaction, but no frenzy, and definitely no overwhelming desire.

Certainly nothing like this.

This was something she could only pray would continue until she just went up in smoke, because in her heart she sensed that there would be nothing like this again for her, once Marcos became part of her past, her history, rather than her future. Channing had taught her that. Taught her that no matter what she felt, what she planned, she couldn't count on any man. Couldn't count on anything lasting.

So, now that they were finally at this rarefied plateau, she was going to make the most of it. She was going to allow her body to have free rein and just take over.

A cry tore from her throat without any preamble or warning that it was even there, or that anything was building within her. Marcos had made her climax so quickly, she hadn't even realized the sensation was in the offing.

It was her first. Channing, she now vaguely realized, had been neither a patient lover nor a clever one. Marcos was everything that Channing was not.

One minute, Marcos's mouth was teasing the flat of her belly, the next, it was possessing the very core of her. The resulting explosion stole her breath away so completely that for a second she couldn't pull in enough air to sustain herself. She found herself coming perilously close to passing out.

Sheer grit propelled her onward.

And then, employing instincts she'd had no idea she possessed, she brought Marcos up to a fever pitch using her own lips and tongue.

Firebrand. Spitfire. Wildcat.

All inadequate words to describe what she was and what she was doing to him right at this moment. "Surprising him" didn't begin to cover what was going on.

Wendy was making him crazy. Utterly, fantastically, deliciously crazy.

Any second now he'd—

Catching her before the final moment, Marcos dragged her supple, damp body up over his own, exciting them both with the heated contact. He was more than primed and ready.

Then, suddenly reversing their positions, Marcos was over her.

And then in her.

The look of sheer wonder on Wendy's face tugged on his heart and whispered to him that he was on very, very perilous ground here, in imminent danger of losing the one organ he had never lost control of before.

Ever.

Sealing his mouth to hers, he began to move. To rock. Taking her on that most intimate of dances until they both ascended to the uppermost peak. A wild peace found them and then settled over Wendy and him as their hearts pounded together in a harmony all their own.

His arms tightened around her, holding her fast. Holding her to him.

Eventually, as the euphoria receded, Marcos found his breath and then his voice.

"So," he whispered against her ear just before he rolled off her and to her side, "spectacular desserts aren't the only thing you're capable of creating." Beside her now, he slipped an arm beneath Wendy and gathered her close to him, unwilling to completely release her or this wondrous feeling just yet.

She felt him shake his head. "You are a complete mystery to me, Wendy Fortune."

She could feel his smile against her cheek and it created another smile deep inside her. So this was what true contentment felt like, she thought. How had she managed to live without it before?

And how could she have settled for Channing without it?

She strove to hang on to the feeling for as long as humanly possible, realizing that, for all intents and purposes, she had just made love for the very first time, since everything that she had experienced before, with Channing, completely paled in comparison.

The desire to whisper, "I love you," was unbelievably strong.

The desire for self-preservation proved to be just a little bit stronger.

Because she'd said the words once, to Channing, not realizing until this moment what they truly meant. The words had been thrown back at her. Not at that time, but later, when Channing had shed her as if she were last year's ski jacket. He had abandoned her to take up with the woman who shortly thereafter became Mrs. Channing Hurston.

There was another reason she didn't give voice to the sentiment that echoed within her. Marcos undoubtedly heard the words "I love you" all the time. She didn't want to be like all the other women who had passed through his life.

Not because she was naive enough to think that what they had would turn into a relationship—she was finally smarter than that—but because she had her pride. If nothing else, she wanted to be at least a little unique in his eyes. And that meant not saying the L-word. Even if she desperately wanted to.

"Every woman wants to be mysterious," she finally said in response to the observation he'd made that she was an enigma.

Marcos threaded his fingers through her hair, pushing a few wayward strands back from her face. The smile on his lips all but made her melt all over again.

So did what he said next.

"You don't strike me as being like 'every woman,'" he murmured, pressing a kiss to her forehead. And then his lips softly brushed a kiss against each eyelid.

Wendy could feel the fire—never fully extinguished—flaring again.

"You *are* good," she breathed, turning her body in toward his. As excitement began to swiftly build up in her all over again, she nipped the tip of his chin with her teeth, and then her lips.

She heard Marcos suck his breath in and that excited her all over again

As if she needed more fuel.

"Right back at you," he breathed, his voice low and rumbling along her skin.

The next moment, there was no space for words, only actions, as they once again embarked on the wild, heady roller coaster ride without brakes that they'd just experienced.

Joy vibrated through Wendy. She'd just bought herself another trip to paradise and pushed back the inevitable for a while longer.

Chapter 15

He couldn't sleep.

Contentment warred with fear. Fear *existed* because of the contentment.

Marcos suppressed a sigh as he carefully leaned back against the headboard. He'd never been in this place before, never felt this way before. Hadn't known *how* something like this could even begin to feel until he was hip-deep in it.

The disappointment he'd been hoping for last week had never materialized. Making love with Wendy had not just lived up to expectations, high though they were, it had exceeded all expectations.

And, as exhilarating as this feeling was, that was how frightening it was, as well.

He was in big trouble and he knew it.

Moonlight inched its way in through the bedroom window, softly caressing the face of the sleeping woman beside him.

Wendy.

The ball of fire he'd made love with for the first time a week ago. And every single night since, without realizing that in so doing nothing would ever be the same again.

Oh, Marcos had had his suspicions, but he'd discounted them and forged on anyway, thinking that the pattern would ultimately remain the same: his interest would wane with each intimate encounter until it eventually disappeared.

Except that it hadn't.

Instead of waning, the feeling, the *need* for her, only seemed to intensify. Which was what scared the hell out of him—he felt consumed by this feeling that she'd generated. Consumed by the desire to be with this woman *all* the time.

He was addicted to Wendy's smile, to the very sight of her. Moreover, he *cared* about her. That was the strongest word he could bring himself to use.

It wasn't just the attraction that kept him a prisoner. Marcos realized that he cared about how she felt, what she thought, what she did. Cared about whether or not she was happy.

He cared.

He'd always treated the women in his life with respect, but there had never been this overwhelming *attachment* that had embedded its hooks in him the way it had now. And he had no idea when it had happened, only that it had. One moment he was a carefree bachelor, bedding yet another desirable woman, the next, he wasn't thinking about any woman but Wendy. Wasn't *wanting* any woman but her.

He had to put an end to this. Now. Before he sank so deeply into the quicksand, there would be no getting free. Ever.

Very slowly, so as not to rouse Wendy, Marcos got out of the queen-size bed. Gathering together the clothes he'd shed so haphazardly last night, he slipped into the bathroom and quickly got dressed. Except for his shoes. Those he carried, afraid that if they came in contact with the tile, she might hear him.

If Wendy opened those soft brown eyes of hers and looked at him, he knew there would be no leaving. And shortly thereafter he'd be going down for probably the third time. Utterly lost.

There was a pad and pencil by her bed. She'd told him she kept them there in case the ingredients for a new dessert came to her in the middle of the night. He took the pencil now and hastily wrote her a note, saying he had to get an early start on the day and hadn't wanted to wake her.

The latter was the truth, but the former bent the edges of that concept. It wasn't the day he was getting an early start on. It was his escape.

Marcos left the note on the pillow next to her. Holding his breath in addition to his shoes, he let himself out of her bedroom, her apartment and, if all went according to his hastily conceived plan, very possibly her life, as well.

Wendy stared at Enrique later that morning, trying to process what he had just said to her. She'd felt rather dazed and confused ever since she'd woken up this morning to find herself alone in bed. Calling out to Marcos, she only heard her own voice echoing back to her, compounding the emptiness.

The moment she'd seen that his clothes were gone, an uneasy feeling had settled in the pit of her stomach. Finding his note on the pillow hadn't helped any. Neither had coming into work only to be told that he wasn't here and wouldn't be for a while.

She had a very bad feeling about this.

"Los Angeles?" she asked Enrique incredulously. Wendy blinked. Why hadn't he mentioned anything about this to her last night? He must have known he was leaving. "What is Marcos doing in Los Angeles?"

"He called me this morning and said he had some business to take care of." Enrique knew his answer probably only raised more questions for her. "Marcos said he was leaving me temporarily in charge."

A chill ran down her back. She should have seen this coming, she upbraided herself.

"How long is 'temporarily'?" Wendy did her best not to look or sound like someone whose feelings had just been slashed.

Enrique shrugged. "Probably only a couple of days or so," he speculated quickly, seeing the flash of hurt in Wendy's eyes. "He said it had something to do with the restaurant," Enrique felt compelled to add, even though the words were his and not Marcos's. The restaurant manager hadn't explained anything at all about the impromptu trip.

Wendy was barely aware of nodding. Everything inside of her felt momentarily numb and disjointed. "Thanks for telling me."

When she'd found herself alone in her apartment this morning, she'd quickly gotten ready and left for work, expecting to see Marcos's car in the lot. But the parking space was empty. Still, she held on to hope, thinking perhaps he had taken a cab here for some reason, or had someone drop him off. Maybe his car was in the shop. Maybe—

Maybe she was being a gullible fool, Wendy told herself angrily.

Marcos hadn't said anything about needing to go in early today, much less going out of town. There was a reason for that, she thought. This had to do with them, not Red.

Her heart felt like lead in her chest as she returned to the table where she normally did her work. She stared at the canisters of various ingredients, not really seeing them. She was drained. More than that, she felt as if someone had just kicked her in the stomach.

Damn it, why had he pulled this vanishing act on her? She hadn't been counting on forever. She was a big girl and knew better than that. But she *had* thought that they had something special going on. A spark. *Something* that would cause him to treat her like a person rather than a nameless, disposable body in the dark.

Had she done something wrong?

How could he just go away like that without saying a single word to her?

Easy, because there's nothing between you. He enjoyed himself and now he's moved on.

Wendy pressed her lips together, hurt and angry as hell at the same time. She thought of the resignation she'd penned last week. It was still in her purse. She'd done it then so that he would sleep with her. But now it took on a whole different reason for existing.

Maybe she should just give it to Enrique. If Marcos could move on so effortlessly without a backward glance, well, then, so could she.

Not move on, quit, a voice in her head mocked. *Are you going to go back to being a quitter after you've come so far?*

Wendy drew in a shaky breath, trying unsuccessfully to shut the voice out.

And then, suddenly, she squared her shoulders as fire came back into her veins.

No, damn it, she thought abruptly, *I'm not.*

She was through being a quitter. That was the old Wendy. The one who didn't have any real self-esteem to speak of. But she'd evolved past that, she told herself. Not just evolved, she'd developed a talent. For the first time in her life, she was *good* at something other than picking out flattering clothes, and nobody was going to take that away from her. Not even a mercurial man with a lethal mouth and the morals of a degenerate alley cat.

"Something wrong?" Enrique asked sympathetically, coming up behind her.

Wendy had been so engrossed in her internal struggle, she hadn't even heard the chef approaching. Startled, she quickly collected herself, raised her head and flashed him a quick smile.

"No, nothing's wrong. Everything's fine." She used her work as a cover. "I'm just trying to visualize a new dessert, that's all."

"You know," he told her gently, "we can serve something more than once here. You've already come up with more different desserts than most chefs create in a year—if not longer. There is no shame in a rerun," he informed her.

Wendy could see she surprised him by agreeing with him wholeheartedly. "No, there isn't. From now on, why don't we do this? We'll offer one old dessert and one new one on each menu."

Enrique nodded, giving his approval to this new approach. "Sounds good to me." And then he decided to stop sidestepping around the elephant in the room and address it instead. He looked at her with concern. "Are you all right, Wendy?"

"I am terrific," she informed him with genuine enthusiasm.

And she meant it.

She had made up her mind right then and there that she wasn't going anywhere. If Marcos—whenever he *did* come back—wanted her to leave, he was going to have to show her the door himself, then brace himself for one hell of a battle because she wasn't about to quit and run away anymore.

One way or another, she was here to stay and he might as well make his peace with it. And if he didn't, well, that was his problem.

Contrary to what he'd told Enrique when he'd called the chef at his home that morning, Marcos wasn't going to Los Angeles. It was a handy excuse to keep anyone—specifically Wendy—from coming to look for him. Rather than take off for California—or parts unknown—he'd remained in Red Rock. But rather than his own home, he'd gone to stay with Rafe.

Accustomed to his own counsel and working things out for himself, Marcos had to admit that this time around he needed a sounding board. He needed someone near his own age to talk to and help him sort out the confusion that had swallowed him whole.

Because from where he was standing, the turmoil wasn't over yet.

So he'd come to Rafe for some brotherly advice. And, if possible, to be talked out of what he was feeling before he allowed his emotions to make him do something stupid. Something he was afraid he was going to wind up regretting.

Rafe hadn't even tried to hide his surprise at seeing his younger brother on his doorstep. Instead of the confident go-getter he was accustomed to, Marcos looked as if he was carrying the weight of the world on his shoulders.

And it was about to break him.

"Didn't think I'd be seeing you again so soon. Is there a problem with the booking?" He guessed at the first thing that occurred to him.

"The booking?" Marcos echoed blankly.

"For my wedding reception," Rafe prompted.

"Oh." Marcos felt like a fool for forgetting about something so important as his brother's wedding.

"No, no problem," he assured Rafe. "This isn't about you."

Rafe gestured toward an overstuffed, wine-colored armchair. He took a seat opposite it. "What is it about?" he asked, purely for form's sake, having a feeling that the out-of-kilter look in his brother's eyes had to do with a woman. Obviously not an ordinary woman, as he'd never seen Marcos like this before.

"It's about me. And a woman." It was coming out choppy and he didn't want it to. But his eloquent tongue had deserted him—along with his common sense, Marcos silently jeered.

"Does this woman have a name?" Rafe asked.

Marcos debated using a false name, but he hadn't come here to Rafe to lie. It had taken a great deal for him to seek help and he had to be completely truthful if he ever hoped to resolve this in some kind of satisfactory manner.

"Wendy," he finally said. "Her name is Wendy Fortune."

"The albatross *tía* and *tío* saddled you with." At least, that had been the last report he'd received from Marcos.

"Not so much an albatross," Marcos allowed. "She turned out to be rather talented."

"In or out of the restaurant?" Rafe queried.

"Both," Marcos admitted. He took a breath, then let it out. That was followed by another.

"Did you come here to tell me what's wrong, or to hyperventilate?" Rafe wanted to know.

Bracing himself, Marcos began.

The revelation took more than several minutes, with Marcos tripping over his own tongue, something that caught Rafe completely by surprise. Rafe was the older brother, but Marcos was definitely the smoother one, the one who could talk a nightingale out of its feathers. This uncertain Marcos was someone he was not expecting or accustomed to.

Rafe listened and did his best to hold his tongue, even though he wanted to jump in and finish Marcos's sentences for him. It took patience.

Even so, it wasn't easy. When his brother paused, either for breath or because he was finished for the time being, Rafe took his opportunity. He didn't bother hiding his surprise.

"So you're telling me that, completely unintentionally, you've found what everyone in this world is looking for—and you're trying to turn your back on it?" When Marcos made no denial, Rafe assumed that he'd guessed right. His next words caught Marcos off guard. "Are you crazy?" Rafe demanded, stunned. For the life of him, now that he was so deeply in love himself, he couldn't see Marcos's problem. "Do you know how many people never find what you just stumbled onto?"

Marcos lifted his shoulders in a vague shrug and then dropped them.

"No," he lied.

"A lot," his older brother assured him. Rafe sighed, shaking his head. He would have never believed that Marcos could suddenly become so uncertain. "Just what is it that you're afraid of?"

That, at least, he could answer, Marcos thought. "Being trapped."

"That," Rafe said, "is just a cop-out. You can be just as 'trapped' being alone as you can in a relationship. More, actually. And if it's the right relationship," Rafe told him, "you're not trapped at all. You're sheltered."

Marcos was shaken by his brother's words. He'd been so busy trying to escape, he hadn't thought of it that way.

"Is that how you feel about Melina?" he asked.

"That's how I feel," Rafe replied. "That, plus I feel damn lucky. I could have gone my whole life, drifting from one meaningless en-counter to another, never feeling as if I'd made any real contact at all. Instead, with Melina I find that we can talk for hours and never even come close to reaching an end. There's so much more to explore, to learn about each other, even though we've known one another for years."

Rising, he drew closer to Marcos and put an arm around his younger brother's shoulders. "Hey, I know. Love's a scary proposition. But do you know the only thing that's scarier?"

Marcos shook his head. "What?"

"*Not* having love," Rafe said with feeling. His eyes searched Marcos's face. "Do you understand what I'm saying?"

Marcos's sigh was more of a cleansing breath. "Yeah, I think I do."

Rafe's eyes probed deeper into his. "And?" he asked, waiting.

Marcos reflected and laughed shortly. "And I guess I'm an idiot," he admitted. "An idiot for choosing to run away instead of taking advantage of what's right there in front of me."

Rafe grinned broadly, satisfied. "Okay, as long as you know." He gestured toward the door. "Now, get out of here. Some of us have work to do."

"Yeah, we do," Marcos agreed. And he'd

let both his work—and Wendy—slide for too long. "Thanks."

With a nod, Marcos turned to cross to the door and let himself out.

"And, Marcos," Rafe called after him. Marcos paused, looking over his shoulder. Rafe grinned broadly. "Welcome to the club."

Marcos flashed the same grin back at him. "Yeah. Thanks."

Now that he'd made up his mind and finally had his head on straight, Marcos couldn't wait to get back to Red. Back to Wendy.

But an uneasiness gnawed away at his gut. He was afraid that it might already be too late. He knew Wendy, knew the way she reacted. His brush-off might have just made her decide to walk out on this latest venture in her life. After all, she'd certainly done it before.

Hell, she'd already offered to quit because she'd perceived their working together as an obstacle to their *coming* together. But he'd left her bed as if he was abandoning her. There was no telling what was going on in her head. If for some reason she decided that he'd just used her for his own pleasure, then dumped her, she would think nothing of walking away for good.

And whose fault is that? he silently demanded.

Didn't matter whose fault it was, it had to be undone. If she walked out on Red—and him— he was just going to have to work harder at getting her back. Because, now that he thought about it, *really* thought about it, the idea of spending the rest of his life without Wendy left him with an incredibly hollow feeling.

A man couldn't live with that kind of emptiness inside him.

With one eye in the rearview mirror, watching for any sign of the police, Marcos flew through yellow lights and busy intersections, bobbing and weaving from one lane to another, switching as if his car was a bouncing ball, until he finally reached Red.

Feeling suddenly breathless, despite the fact that he hadn't run so much as an inch, Marcos bolted from his sedan and entered the restaurant through the rear double doors.

When he walked into the kitchen, he felt his stomach lurch, then fall.

Wendy wasn't there.

Chapter 16

Okay, now what?

Exiting the medical building, Cooper Fortune frowned as he looked at the DNA report in his hand. He'd picked it up less than five minutes ago at the laboratory that had been steadily ruling out one by one, the various male members of the Fortune family as being baby Anthony's biological father.

Until him.

"We have a winner," Cooper murmured under his breath, still stunned at this newest twist in his life.

He was Anthony's father.

It wasn't that he was too young to be a father. Hell, at forty-one, if anything, he would have said he was too old to be responsible for a four-month-old infant and all that entailed. Besides, he wasn't exactly a pillar of the community. Until Ross had tracked him down, he'd been drifting from state to state, picking up work and women as each came his way. And nothing permanent had ever come of either.

Until now.

Standing outside in the street, Cooper was still having trouble believing it. It all just felt too surreal.

He was a father.

What did he know about being a father? For two cents—less—he could just turn around and disappear again, the way he had for so much of his life.

But there was the kid to think of. Anthony hadn't asked to be born.

Hell, *he* hadn't asked to be a father, either, but the kid really had absolutely no responsibility for being born. And he had already received one blow. He'd been abandoned by his mother. Having his father run out on him as well just didn't seem right.

No matter how much he wanted to put this behind him. Cooper folded the report twice over and stuffed it into his back pocket.

The single word throbbed over and over again in his brain.

Father.

How could such a small word feel so damn heavy? And the label came with strings. He'd never been one for strings, had lived most of his life avoiding them and entanglements in general.

Looks like that's going to have to change, Coop, he told himself.

A lot of things were going to have to change, he thought. Namely his lifestyle. He was going to have to clean up his act, settle down. Find some kind of steady work. It wasn't just him anymore.

Even without a clue about all the things that being a parent involved, he figured he'd have to do a better job than his mother had with the four of them. For all intents and purposes, he, Ross, Flint and Frannie had raised themselves. They'd had to. Their flirt of a mother was too busy charming the pants off whatever man had caught her fancy at the time. Everyone in the family said that Cynthia Fortune had a hell of a track record: four husbands, one of whom at least had had the good sense to die. The others she'd divorced.

He thought of his only sister, the so-called

baby of the family. Frannie had a couple of kids of her own. Maybe she could give him a few pointers and help out a little until he got the hang of all this.

Cooper shook his head as he started walking toward his car. He wasn't one to look into the future. Hell, he hardly even thought beyond the end of the week, a paycheck and being free until Monday. And never once in all that time had he *ever* thought of himself as being someone's father.

Well, he was now.

"Marcos," Enrique exclaimed as he came out of the walk-in refrigerator, "when did you get back?"

The chef had his hands full, carrying a fresh rack of lamb in a large, well-used shallow pan. He set it on the stainless-steel counter and crossed over to Red's manager. Enrique looked genuinely pleased to see him.

But there was only one person's reaction that Marcos cared about.

Rather than explain to the chef that he'd actually never left town, Marcos merely shrugged and murmured a vague, "Just a while ago."

Nodding, Enrique's smile was broad as the man's eyes met his. "Good trip?"

"You might say that."

At least, in the sense that Rafe had made him see things clearly for perhaps the first time in his adult life. But he didn't want to continue talking about the trip that wasn't. There was something far more important that needed his attention.

"Is Wendy here?" Marcos wanted to know, cutting through any more chitchat.

"Right behind you, Marcos."

The second he heard just the first syllable of the melodic Southern drawl, Marcos could feel his heart accelerating. It seemed almost inconceivable to him that the same voice had annoyed him so much just a short while ago.

He swung around to face her only to see that Wendy had already walked over to the table that had become her workstation since she'd taken on the role of pastry chef.

For a moment he just stared at her, drinking in the sight of her. Absorbing every last nuance. She hadn't quit and left town the way he'd been afraid she would. He'd acted like an idiot but she was still here.

Somebody up there had to like him, Marcos thought, as wave after wave of relief washed over him.

"I need to talk to you," he finally said.

She slanted a glance at him as she continued to measure out the ingredients she'd decided she was going to need in concocting today's dessert. Cups and measuring spoons began lining up like tiny confectionary soldiers.

"Talk fast, then," she instructed matter-of-factly. "I've got a lot of things to do."

He glanced toward Enrique. So far, because of the early hour, the chef was still the only other occupant in the kitchen.

"I need to talk to you alone," Marcos qualified.

Part of her just wanted to throw her arms around him, to hold on to him and that exhilaration she'd felt when she'd walked in and seen the back of his head. When she knew he'd come back and was asking for her, instead of stretching out his vanishing act.

The other part of her wanted to hit him upside his head and demand to know why he'd left her bed like that to begin with. Why he'd made her feel as if she didn't matter.

She compromised. Didn't hug, didn't hit. Instead, she stood her ground and continued working.

"Then I'm afraid it's going to have to wait," she answered, pouring powdered sugar, all but lighter than air, into a glass measuring cup.

She made a judgment call and used a little more than three quarters of a cup. "The lunch crowd is going to be coming soon and I'm still not sure what I'm putting on the dessert menu."

"I would stay out of her way if I were you," Enrique advised. "She's been a little dynamo since you 'left on business.'"

His tone caught Marcos's attention. Did Enrique know, or just suspect, that he hadn't gone anywhere? Or was he just being paranoid?

Either way, he needed the man to absent himself for a few minutes. "Can you give us a minute, Enrique?" he requested.

"I can give you five," Enrique countered. "But after that, I need to get started myself. This rack of lamb is not going to prepare itself."

A minute later, the door leading to the main dining area closed again.

He and Wendy were alone.

Marcos had no idea where to begin. He'd never been at a loss for words before. But Wendy had changed a lot of things in his life. And now he realized that he wanted her to continue changing them. Wanted her to stay in his life.

So he pushed forward, saying the first thing

that came to his mind. He needed to apologize, to accept blame where blame was due.

"You're angry, I get that."

You don't know the half of it, Wendy thought. But to admit that would be to give him more control over her than she was willing to relinquish.

So instead she said, "What I am, Marcos, is busy. You might have left Enrique in charge when you went off on your little trip to L.A., but I'm the one who's been picking up the slack, doing double duty in the kitchen and out there in the dining area. If what you have to say is *really* important, I'd appreciate you holding your tongue until after we close, when I can give you my full attention."

With that, Wendy moved past him to the refrigerator. She was going to need chilled heavy cream for this one.

She'd just reached the stainless-steel door when Marcos spoke again, addressing the words to her back. "I love you."

Wendy froze. She couldn't have heard him right. That had to be her ears playing tricks on her.

Still, she couldn't just continue walking away from him, doing what she was doing, without verifying what she'd just *thought* she'd heard.

Very slowly, she turned around to look at him, telling her heart it had no business lodging itself in her throat.

"What did you say?" The words came out in a hoarse whisper.

He wanted to take a step closer to her, but he remained where he was. For now it was enough that she wasn't walking away from him.

"I said I love you."

Okay, what kind of a game *was* he playing? "Just like that?"

He didn't want her thinking that he'd said that to every woman who'd come into his life. Because he hadn't. Not even once. She needed to understand that.

"No, not just like that," Marcos told her. "Those words don't come easy to me. Hell, they don't come at all."

Disbelief fought with a new surge of joy. She knew she should just contradict him. After all, so many men used that line to soften up the women who caught their momentary fancy. Used those words to get what they wanted from a woman.

But the more she thought about it, the more she realized that Marcos was telling her the truth. Never once had he said or even murmured that term of endearment. Or any other term of endearment, for that matter.

She was the one who had almost blurted it out that first night, but she'd managed to stop herself just in time.

"So why are those words coming now?" she asked Marcos quietly.

This wasn't going to be easy, he thought. But then, something real, something lasting, normally wasn't easy. Because "easy" didn't count.

"Because I wanted you to know what I was feeling," he told her honestly. "Wanted you to know that I left because of that feeling."

He had just lost her. Wendy shook her head. "That doesn't make sense."

"It does to me." Feeling on slightly safer ground, very slowly, he crossed to her, cutting the distance an inch at a time. Letting what was happening, what he was saying, sink in for her as well as himself. "I left because you scared the hell out of me. I'd never felt that for any woman before and it made me feel vulnerable. Exposed. Naked."

She smiled and her eyes lit up with the warmth that she was suddenly feeling. "I like that image. Naked," she qualified, "not vulnerable or exposed." She didn't want him to feel either.

Now Marcos could feel himself smiling, as well. "I can do naked."

"Not here you can't," she cautioned with a straight face. "I'd wind up being killed in the stampede."

He laughed. "I was thinking more along the lines of at home, in our bedroom."

The description hit her a moment after he'd said it. This time she *knew* she had to be hearing things.

"Back up," she instructed him. He raised a quizzical eyebrow, waiting for her to elaborate. "*Our* bedroom?" she questioned, emphasizing the first word.

"That's what I said," he agreed. Did she have a problem with that? He was making plans for them, but what if they weren't *her* plans? "Something wrong?"

"Not wrong, exactly, but did I miss something?" she asked. "Just when did we go from 'yours' to 'ours'?"

He'd gotten ahead of himself, he realized.

"We didn't," Marcos admitted, slipping his arms around her and drawing her closer to him. "Yet. But I'm hoping we will. Once you say yes."

Ordinarily she was the speedy one, but this was going way too fast for her to keep up. She had deliberately refrained from spinning the same kind of dreams about Marcos that she had once had about Channing. Refrained because she was afraid of having her hopes dashed and her heart broken.

The heartbreak would be her first—she realized now that she had never really loved Channing. And, since she hadn't loved him, then he hadn't broken her heart when he'd suddenly announced he was leaving her.

All he'd done was injure her pride. Pride had a way of recovering.

She was trying to make sense of what Marcos was saying, to prevent suddenly finding that she had walked off a cliff like some cartoon character.

"Are you asking me to move in with you?"

Marcos inclined his head. Not wanting to be disappointed, he was still feeling her out. "In a way, yes."

Now she was confused. Maybe she was reading more into this than he'd meant. "In what way?" she wanted to know.

Okay, here goes everything, he thought, taking a breath and plunging into the deep end of the pool. No more net.

His eyes never left her face as he said, "Well, I was raised to believe that husbands and wives were supposed to live together."

She was still confused. "What does that have to do with— Wait!" she cried, suddenly stunned more than she thought possible. "Wait," she repeated, pressing her hand against his chest as if to physically keep any more words from coming out until she succeeded in untangling the ones already spoken. "Are you saying what I think you're saying?"

But even as she began to ask, Wendy knew she had to be making a mistake. A mistake she desperately wanted to be true.

"Are you asking me to marry you, Marcos?"

He nodded his head. "Yes."

Wendy surprised him by swinging and cuffing him on the back of the head. "Ow!" he cried in protest.

But before he could ask her what that had been for, she said, "Well, then, do it. Ask me already, don't just go through the motions."

She wasn't going to say no, he thought, relieved. He felt as if he could leap up and touch the moon. "Wendy Fortune, will you marry me?"

She wanted to believe this was happening,

she really did. But once burned, twice wary—wasn't that the saying? "You're serious?"

What did it take to make her believe him? "Would you like me to write it in blood?" Even as he offered, Marcos began rolling up his right sleeve.

"No!" she cried, grabbing his arm. "What I'd like is for you to kiss me."

"*After* you answer my question," he told her.

She looked stunned. Was there even a question what her answer would be? Hadn't she already made herself clear about that?

"Yes," she cried. "Of course I'll marry you. I've been in love with you practically from the first time you scowled at me. How could you even think I'd say no?"

"Because you're unpredictable." God, but he loved this woman. And he would go on loving her until the last breath in his body was gone. "And I'm looking forward to spending the rest of my life being surprised," he told her.

"Whatever you say." Wendy wound her arms around his neck and leaned her body into his, just as his mouth began to come down on hers.

But not before Marcos responded, "I'll hold you to that."

She didn't care. "Just as long as you go on holding me," she murmured.

"Happy to oblige," Marcos told her, sealing his mouth to hers.

"Okay, your five minutes are up," Enrique announced, walking back into the kitchen.

Neither Wendy nor Marcos appeared to hear him or even realize that he had walked back into the room.

He took one look, nodded and backed out. "Maybe I'll give you five more minutes," Enrique allowed with a wide grin.

* * * * *

DIANA PALMER COLLECTION

SAVE 30% AND GET A FREE GIFT!

Cowboys, ranchers, lawmen. Bestselling author Diana Palmer combines hunky heroes and the American West in sizzling stories of love. Hold onto your heart because these strong-willed, handsome cowboys are ready to find love.

YES! Please send me the first shipment of three books from the **Diana Palmer Collection**. If I do not cancel, I will receive one more shipment, about a month later, consisting of three 2-in-1 books, and I will be billed at the same discount price of $16.78 U.S./$20.98 CAN., plus $1.50 for shipping and handling.* That's a 30% discount off the cover prices! Plus, I'll receive a FREE stunning horseshoe pendant necklace (approx. retail value of $14.99)!

☐ 284 HCN 4332   ☐ 484 HCN 4332

Name (please print)

Address   Apt. #

City   State/Province   Zip/Postal Code

Mail to the **Reader Service:**
IN U.S.A.: P.O. Box 1867, Buffalo, NY. 14240-1867
IN CANADA: P.O. Box 609, Fort Erie, Ontario L2A 5X3

Get 4 FREE REWARDS!

We'll send you 2 FREE Books plus 2 FREE Mystery Gifts.

Harlequin® Special Edition books feature heroines finding the balance between their work life and personal life on the way to finding true love.

FREE
Value Over
$20

Get 4 FREE REWARDS!

We'll send you 2 FREE Books plus 2 FREE Mystery Gifts.

Harlequin® Heartwarming™ Larger-Print books feature traditional values of home, family, community and—most of all—love.

FREE Value Over $20

YES! Please send me 2 FREE Harlequin® Heartwarming™ Larger-Print novels and my 2 FREE mystery gifts (gifts worth about $10 retail). After receiving them, if I don't wish to receive any more books, I can return the shipping statement marked "cancel." If I don't cancel, I will receive 4 brand-new larger-print novels every month and be billed just $5.49 per book in the U.S. or $6.24 per book in Canada. That's a savings of at least 19% off the cover price. It's quite a bargain! Shipping and handling is just 50¢ per book in the U.S. and 75¢ per book in Canada.* I understand that accepting the 2 free books and gifts places me under no obligation to buy anything. I can always return a shipment and cancel at any time. The free books and gifts are mine to keep no matter what I decide.

161/361 IDN GMY3

Name (please print)

Address   Apt. #

City   State/Province   Zip/Postal Code

Mail to the **Reader Service:**
IN U.S.A.: P.O. Box 1341, Buffalo, NY 14240-8531
IN CANADA: P.O. Box 603, Fort Erie, Ontario L2A 5X3

Want to try 2 free books from another series? Call 1-800-873-8635 or visit www.ReaderService.com.

READERSERVICE.COM

Manage your account online!

- Review your order history
- Manage your payments
- Update your address

We've designed the Reader Service website just for you.

Enjoy all the features!

- Discover new series available to you, and read excerpts from any series.
- Respond to mailings and special monthly offers.
- Browse the Bonus Bucks catalog and online-only exculsives.
- Share your feedback.

Visit us at:
ReaderService.com